Milo March is a hard-drinking, womanizing, wisecracking, James-Bondian character. He always comes out on top through a combination of personality, bluff, bravado, luck, skill, experience, and intellect. He is a shrewd judge of human character, a crack shot, and a deeper character than I have found in most of the other spy/thriller novels I've read. But, above all, he is a con-man—and a very good one. It is Milo March himself who makes the series worth reading.

—Don Miller, *The Mystery Nook* fanzine 12

Steeger Books is proud to reissue twenty-three vintage novels and stories by M.E. Chaber, whose Milo March Mysteries deliver mile-a-minute action and breezily readable entertainment for thriller buffs.

Milo is an Insurance Investigator who takes on the tough cases. Organized crime, grand theft, arson, suspicious disappearances, murders, and millions and millions of dollars—whatever it is, Milo is just the man for the job. Or even the only man for it.

During World War II, Milo was assigned to the OSS and later the CIA. Now in the Army Reserves, with the rank of Major, he is recalled for special jobs behind the Iron Curtain. As an agent, he chops necks, trusses men like chickens to steal their uniforms, shoots point blank at secret police—yet shows compassion to an agent from the other side.

Whatever Milo does, he knows how to do it right. When the work is completed, he returns to his favorite things: women, booze, and good food, more or less in that order....

THE MILO MARCH MYSTERIES

Hangman's Harvest

No Grave for March

The Man Inside

As Old as Cain

The Splintered Man

A Lonely Walk

The Gallows Garden

A Hearse of Another Color

So Dead the Rose

Jade for a Lady

Softly in the Night

Uneasy Lies the Dead

Six Who Ran

Wanted: Dead Men

The Day It Rained Diamonds

A Man in the Middle

Wild Midnight Falls

The Flaming Man

Green Grow the Graves

The Bonded Dead

Born to Be Hanged

Death to the Brides

The Twisted Trap: Six Milo March Stories

Wild Midnight Falls

KENDELL FOSTER CROSSEN
Writing as
M.E. CHABER

With an Afterword by
KENDRA CROSSEN BURROUGHS

STEEGER BOOKS / **2021**

PUBLISHED BY STEEGER BOOKS
Visit steegerbooks.com for more books like this.

PUBLISHING HISTORY

Hardcover
New York: Holt, Rinehart & Winston (A Rinehart Suspense Novel), August 1968. Dust jacket by James McMullan.
Toronto: Holt, Rinehart & Winston of Canada, 1968.
Roslyn, NY: Detective Book Club #318, Walter J. Black, Inc., October 1968. (With *Fuzz* by Ed McBain and *A Taste of Sangria* by Carlton Keith.)

Paperback
New York: Paperback Library (63-265), A Milo March Mystery, #5, February 1970. Cover by Robert McGinnis.

ISBN: 978-1-61827-571-4

For Maria Louisa Eleni Palmieri Magazu Crossen—whose
lovely facets far outnumber her names

What will you say when the world is dying?
What, when the last wild midnight falls
Dark, too dark for the bat to be flying
Round the ruins of old St. Paul's?

—Alfred Noyes, *Tales of the Mermaid Tavern*

CONTENTS

POTPOURRI

The young, hard-faced American tossed on the bare floor of the cell and then screamed at the darkness that closed in on his mind. The sound of his own voice awakened him and he sat up, angered by the weakness that struck when he was asleep. There was still nothing but darkness, but this was real and not something in his mind, and it did not frighten him. It was always dark in the cell, and he had no idea whether it was day or night—not that it made any difference. He wished he had a cigarette, but even that hunger had been dulled by time.

Finally he stood up and reached over to the wall, running his hand along it until he felt the marks he'd made. He thought that they brought him food twice a day. At least they brought coffee and bread; then later what tasted like watery cabbage soup, more bread, and tea. After that it was coffee and bread again. Once, a guard had forgotten to take the spoon when he came for the bowl. The American had sharpened the handle on the stone walls and after that always made a mark on the wall each time he was given coffee and bread. There were now sixty-one marks. He counted them again to be sure. Then his hand slipped down to where he had scratched his name.

James Hartwell. It gave him substance, which was often on the verge of vanishing in the prison. And someday someone might see it and the information would travel back across the ocean and close an open file. He expected no more. The prospect of a cell like this and then death was a part of his profession.

After a while he curled up on the floor again and went back to sleep. The guards had to shake him awake when they brought his coffee and bread. They did not speak, for they knew that he understood their language.

Grigory Masinov was one of the new Soviet men. He had been born after the Revolution and had never known any form of society other than that in the Soviet Union. He was a loyal Russian.

He was also a cynic. He saw no great conflict in these two positions. He had become a member of the secret police while he was still at university. He had advanced in his profession until, at the age of thirty-four, he was a member of the KGB with a rating equivalent to that of a sergeant in the Red Army. He was trusted. He had been part of a security guard on trips to the United States, France, England, and Yugoslavia. For six months he had been assigned to the Soviet delegation to the United Nations. It was sometime during this period that Grigory became a cynic. But that was not the way that he saw himself. He was a realist, in a Marxist sense, about mankind as well as systems.

He went ahead, carefully setting a trap for the man he was supposed to watch, but his thoughts were really on his future.

Marya Rijekta undressed quickly in the tiny bathroom and

glanced down at her body. It was a beautiful body, unmarred by wrinkles or fat, smooth and full, accented by the coral-tipped breasts and the triangle of red-gold hair. How long, she thought, would it look like this? She ran her fingers through her long, blond hair and walked into the other room where the man waited impatiently. She glanced automatically at the chandelier where the microphone was hidden. There was always a microphone, she thought bitterly, although it was not always the property of the same people. She wondered what it would be like to make love in a room where there were no microphones.

The microphone faithfully recorded the creak of the bed and the heavy breathing of the man. It failed to catch the inaudible sigh of Marya Rijekta or the expression in her eyes as she stared up at the chandelier.

Josip Voukelitch was merely one of many journalists sitting in the large room listening to the remarks of the Soviet Premier and making notes in two neat columns. One column would end up in a special bureau, where it would be analyzed for the benefit of Tito. The other would end up in another special bureau thousands of miles away. Voukelitch was bored. It was his normal state.

Irina Simonov a attended this same news conference and would later write a story for *Pravda*. She didn't have to take notes. She had a copy of the speech, and if there was any departure from the text the additions would be waiting for her when she reached the office. Irina was also bored, although her outward appearance was that of any attractive woman of twenty-five from almost any country. Irina carried a dream deep within her, but it was now more than two months since she had been able to do anything about it. She wasn't certain why this was true and didn't think too much about it. She knew it was an area where thinking was dangerous.

James Hartwell, Grigory Masinov, Marya Rijekta, Josip Voukelitch, Irina Simonova—they were all quite different from each other, yet they shared one thing in common. Each one of them existed in his or her own prison, real or imagined, yet not one of them knew or for that matter cared about any of the others. And there were two men, unknown to any of them, who would soon start moving them as if they were puppets on strings.

One of these men was sitting in a large office in the Kremlin. It was a special office, known to only a few and inspiring fear in most of them. The man who sat there and pulled his thousands of strings, stretching all over the world, had once been famous, but it was believed that he had died more than twenty years earlier in a Japanese prison. He was now in his seventies; his hair white and his face lined with the passions and cruelties that had filled his life. He pressed a button on his desk and waited. The soldier who entered saluted and stood at attention.

"Hartwell?" the old man asked.

"He has not yet broken," the soldier replied. "Perhaps it is time for stronger measures."

The old man studied him. "Would stronger measures break you, Nikolai?"

Something like fear came into the soldier's eyes. "Of course not," he said quickly. "But I am different."

"No, you're not," the old man said quietly. "Hartwell is also a professional. He would die with the same quietness that marked his work until we were lucky enough to catch him. Notice that I said *luck*, Nikolai. It was luck. The next time it must be skill. Move Hartwell to another cell. Feed him better—but not too much better. Have him watched, but leave him alone. Hartwell will become our prize cheese."

"Yes, sir," the soldier said, but he sounded puzzled.

"Sooner or later a hungry mouse will come looking for cheese, and there he will be."

"Then why not show him off in a public trial?"

The old man shook his head. "You've been listening to our propaganda again, Nikolai. I've warned you about that before. They are not stupid. They will find him. But if we make it easy for them, they will merely write him off and forget about it. We have plenty of time. Impatience, my dear comrade, is the cardinal sin of our profession. Try to remember that."

The soldier saluted and left.

And there was yet another man in New York City...

ONE

Up to a point it was like every other morning. I went to my office on Madison Avenue in New York City and opened the mail. It was mostly bills, but somebody did want me to give money to a worthy cause and somebody else wanted me to subscribe to the *Wall Street Journal*. I made out checks for the bills and threw the other things into the wastebasket.

There wasn't anything else for me to do at the moment, so I went to the file cabinet and got out a bottle of V.O., poured myself a small drink, and sipped it, wishing the phone would ring. That was my first mistake.

I'm March. Milo March. I have a couple of pieces of paper that say I'm a private detective, but I work as an insurance investigator. At least that's the way I make my living. Most of my work comes from a single company, although I occasionally work for one of the others.

The phone rang. I thought it might mean a job. I snatched up the receiver and said hello.

"March?" a voice asked.

"Yes," I said. That was my second mistake.

"I'm calling for your Uncle Bobby," the man said. "You are to be in the bar of the Holson Hotel on Madison Avenue at eight o'clock tonight." He hung up.

I replaced the receiver and cursed. I poured myself another

drink and stared moodily at it. The phone call meant nothing but trouble.

Once upon a time I had spent several years in the United States Army. I had been assigned to the OSS and then, later, to the CIA. I was still in the Reserves, with the rank of Major, and had been recalled several times to do a special job for the agency. Usually they just recalled me and then ordered me on to a job. They were using a different tactic this time. "Uncle Bobby" was the code name for General Sam Roberts, an important man in the CIA.

As far as I was concerned, the day was shot anyway, so I locked the office and left. I went downtown to my favorite restaurant, the Blue Mill, and worked over some martinis and talked to Alcino until it was lunchtime.

After lunch I went home, which was only a few blocks away, on Perry Street. I checked with my answering service, but there hadn't been any more calls. So I said to hell with it and took a nap. I'd been up late the night before.

I walked into the bar at the Holson Hotel at exactly eight o'clock. There were only a few people in the bar, and General Roberts was not one of them. I didn't expect him to be there. He was usually trickier than that. I took a stool at some distance from the other drinkers and ordered a martini. A few minutes later another man entered and sat on the second stool away from me. I glanced at him. He looked like any eager young executive, and he wasn't paying any attention to me.

I was watching the mirror in back of the bar. I could see behind me through the entrance to the lobby; I figured the General or one of his trained seals might come from that direction. I didn't see the General, but I did see somebody else who caught my attention. She was tall and blond and beautiful. She walked through the lobby with a swing that must have caused tremors in every earthquake center in the country.

"Beautiful, isn't she?" a voice asked. It was the man who had taken a stool near me.

"I guess so," I said shortly. I turned back to my martini.

"Merry Sanders," he said conversationally. "Thirty-six, twenty-four, thirty-six.

Calls herself a model. Price: one hundred dollars a night and, I'm told, worth every cent of it."

This time I really looked at him, and began to revise my opinion. "Really?" I asked. "Are you her pimp?"

He didn't like that, but his only reaction was a slight tightening of the muscles around his mouth. "No. Besides, it's not necessary. She's already booked for the night."

"That's nice. What are you selling? Peeping privileges through the keyhole in the adjoining suite?" I was deliberately being as insulting as I could.

The muscles tightened a little more. "No, but you might be interested to know where she's going."

"All right," I said wearily, "I'll play your little game. Where is she going?"

"To a suite on the fifth floor," he said. He was still not looking at me, paying strict attention to his drink and speaking very softly.

"The suite was rented by you three days ago. You asked for the girl for tonight through her regular answering service. She is probably in the bedroom by now, getting ready for you."

"And it's not even Christmas," I said. "Is there an explanation for this, or are you just talking?"

"The girl is in the bedroom waiting for you. Uncle Bobby is in the living room waiting for you. And there are people in and around the hotel who are watching you and have been since you arrived at eight o'clock."

"I must be getting old," I said, sighing. "I should have smelled you when you first came in. Any other tasty little bits of information for me?"

"You rented the suite under the name of Peter Miloff three days ago. I believe there is some mail for you at the desk. You won't need a key to get in. The door to the suite is unlocked. That's all."

"Not quite. You didn't tell me the number of the suite."

He flushed. "Five twelve." He turned slightly away from me.

I smiled to myself and finished my martini. Then I walked into the lobby and took the elevator to the fifth floor.

I found the suite without any trouble. I had known the General for a long time and was familiar with the way he liked to set up little traps for his men, just to be sure they were on their toes. I took my gun from its shoulder holster and gently tried the doorknob. As soon as I knew it would open, I moved into the room fast.

General Roberts was sitting in a chair, a drink in his left hand and a gun in his right. But the gun was pointed in the wrong direction. He started to lift it, then realized he was too late.

I shut the door behind me. "Just wanted to see if you were on your toes, sir," I said.

He reddened. "I see that time has not made you any more respectful," he growled. "All right. Put it away. And you'd better go tell the young lady in the next room that you have some business to take care of before you can see her. She's liable to get curious hearing voices in here."

I put the gun away and went to what was obviously the bedroom door. I tapped on it gently and then opened it. She had already changed into something soft and transparent. I had to admit that she was quite a vision.

"Hi, honey," I said.

"Hi," she said. "You mean you're my customer?"

"It looks like it."

"You mean I get lucky for once."

"Thanks," I told her. "I have to talk some business in the next room for a few minutes. Make yourself at home. If you want anything from room service, order it and sign my name."

"Champagne?" she asked hopefully.

"Anything you want, baby. But if you get it, you'd better throw on a robe so the waiter doesn't have a heart attack."

She laughed, and I went back to the other room.

The General looked at me sourly and waved to a small bar. "We ordered the things that you seem to like."

"How kind of you," I said. I went over and looked. There was gin and vermouth and V.O. I mixed myself a martini and went back to sit across from him.

"Things have certainly changed," I said. "It used to be that I was ordered back into uniform when you wanted something and then given orders. Now, suddenly, I have a hotel suite, a lot of free booze, and a hundred-dollar whore. What would the taxpayers say?"

He cleared his throat nervously. "This is a special situation," he said. "I feel that it is safer for you if you are not back in uniform for this assignment. I am therefore asking you to volunteer. If you refuse, I will then have no choice but to have you recalled to active duty."

"Let's hear about it," I said. "I gather that was your trained seal down in the bar?"

"He is one of my men, yes."

"He said something about me being watched since I arrived at the hotel. Who's doing the watching?"

"Soviet personnel."

"Why?"

"It is slightly complicated," he said. "A few months ago an important Russian trade official came to America. Among other things, he attended a trade showing of coin vending machines. The show was held in Chicago. During it, he had several meetings with one of the officers of a firm known as the Brotherhood Coin Vending Company. He was very interested in all types of vending machines. Sometime after he returned to the Soviet Union, he requested the Brotherhood company to recommend a vending machine specialist who might be hired by the Russian government for a period of six months, subject to the approval of the State Department here."

"Who owns the vending machine company in Chicago?"

"The Syndicate."

"I thought maybe that's what that 'brotherhood' jazz meant. So what did they do about it?"

"They recommended a specialist. His name is Peter Miloff."

I started to ask a question, then stopped. I suddenly remembered what the man downstairs had said. He'd mentioned that I had rented this suite three days ago, and that it was rented in the name of Peter Miloff.

"As if I didn't know," I said casually, "who is Peter Miloff?"

He gave me what passed for a smile in the upper ranks. "You are, my dear Milo."

"Isn't that sweet? Does the Syndicate know who Peter Miloff is?"

"Only that he is someone that we want sent to Russia."

"And they agreed just like that? Since when did you get so chummy with the Syndicate?"

"It's really very simple. First, they like to think of themselves as patriotic Americans when it comes to international politics. It's very silly, although they did make one important contribution to the invasion of Europe during the last war."*

I gave a simple, four-letter word summation of my opinion of that.

"Secondly," he continued, "we are in a position to put certain pressures on an individual group such as this that could not be used by the regular law enforcement agencies. The Syndicate notified another Federal agency when they were first approached by the Russians. This information was passed along to us through channels."

---

* The Mafia aided the Allied invasion of Sicily in 1943. (All footnotes were added by the editor.)

"How else?"

He flushed. "We talked to them, and they were glad to suggest you as the specialist. As it now stands, you've been working for them for slightly more than two years at a very good salary. Their records will bear this out. There are also records proving that you have lived in one apartment in Chicago for the same period of time. We have provided you with complete identification and a history covering your entire life. You will find all of it in a file in the dresser drawer. I suggest that you memorize it."

"You've gone to a lot of trouble without knowing whether I'll do the job for you or not."

"You'll do it," he said grimly, "one way or the other."

"Charm was always one of your weak spots, General," I told him. "Where did you dig up this name Peter Miloff for me?"

"Well, Miloff is close enough to your real first name, so you shouldn't have too much trouble responding to it from the beginning. And according to your records, you are a third-generation American of Russian ancestry. This will help explain your familiarity with the language."

"What happens if the Russians don't go for this after you've spent so much time on it?"

"They already have gone for it. They have made their request to the State Department, and I have good reason to believe that one of your two letters down at the desk is also from the Russians. It was delivered this afternoon by hand by a Russian. The other letter contains your paycheck from the Brotherhood company."

"What do I do with that?"

"Spend it. We've given them the money. They're not that patriotic."

"Well," I said, "it seems to leave only one small question. I realize that it's unimportant, but I do feel compelled to ask it."

"What?"

"What do we do about the fact that the only thing I know about a coin vending machine is that you put coins into it, then push buttons or pull levers, and something comes out of it or two lemons show up and you shrug. I doubt if that will satisfy even the most backward Russian."

"That's no problem," he said airily. "A Mr. Benotti is the owner of the Brotherhood company. You might call him wealthy. He owns what he calls a camp on a lake in Upstate New York, but I understand it has all the comforts of home. It is also remote and boasts a very large collection of vending machines. You are going to spend a two-week vacation there before going on your Russian trip."

"That's a nice touch," I said. "The trusted and valuable associate who gets the use of the family castle. Do I get a well-deserved rest on this vacation?"

"You do not. You will go through a crash program on the subject of vending machines. By the end of the two weeks you should be able to give the Russians sound advice on how to build and operate machines which will dispense food, hot tea, and various small articles that the citizens might wish to purchase without lining up in front of a store."

"What about a nice cup of vodka?"

He ignored me. "You will also be briefed on your assignment in Russia. The Russians will probably follow you to the camp and maintain a watch on it while you are there. Mr. Benotti's chauffeur will be in residence for your convenience and lives in an apartment over the garage. He is also the expert who will instruct you about vending machines. He has been carefully checked out. Some of our personnel will already be in the house when you arrive, and will, naturally, stay out of sight while you are there."

"And when do I take this vacation?"

"In four or five days, depending somewhat on the results of your meeting with the Russian officials. You will tell them that you came here on business for the company and that your vacation was already planned. You intend to take it before going on to anything else. You'll go to your apartment in Chicago from here, then from there back to New York to the camp. You will undoubtedly be followed."

"Won't they check on the Chicago apartment?"

"I'm sure they will, but it will check out. Mr. Benotti also owns that building."

"Strange bedfellows," I murmured. "Do the Russians know who they're dealing with?"

"I'm sure they do. But they're practical fellows, and when they want help, they want the best."

"And does your Mr. Benotti know who this Peter Miloff is?"

"You mean does he know you're Milo March? No."

"General," I said, "you always manage to put me in such interesting situations. My erstwhile employer belongs to a group who would love to get Milo March. They are loaning me out to a group of people who would love to get Milo March."

"My boy, I have confidence in you."

"I'll try to remember that when they shoot me," I said. "What do I do, now that I'm going to be followed, about getting any of my clothes out of my real apartment?"

"No problem. We naturally know your size and your taste in clothes. You will find quite a bit of clothing here and two fine pieces of luggage. You will find more in the apartment in Chicago." He squinted at me. "I see you're carrying a gun. I suggest that you give it to me to keep until you return from Russia. You'll find a very good gun in the dresser. It's registered to Peter Miloff in Chicago and there's a permit for it. I also suggest that you give me all of your personal papers and substitute the ones that are here."

I took out the gun and gave it to him. Then I removed everything that identified me as Milo March and handed these over. I felt as if I were walking naked on the street. He put everything away in a briefcase.

"I guess," he said, "that's about it for now. We'll give you the rest at the camp. As soon as you know when you will go to the camp, phone the special number. Benotti's man will pick you up at the apartment. In the left-hand drawer of the dresser you will find the key to this suite and the key to your Chicago apartment, plus the address of that apartment, which is on your identification papers. If you want anything from your own place, tell us when you call the special number, and we'll see that those things are transferred to your Chicago apartment while you're at the camp."

"I haven't agreed to do it yet," I said.

His eyebrows went up. "You mean I have to have you recalled to active duty, Major?"

"I'll do it," I said, "but I just don't like to be taken for granted. I may be a floozy, but I'm my own floozy. Let us keep that clearly in mind, General."

He cleared his throat. "Just wanted the issue to be clear. Well, I'd better be going."

"Just one more thing, General," I said gently. "You haven't told me what you expect me to do in Russia, besides telling them how to build a machine that will spit out a doughnut if someone deposits a kopeck."

"Only two things," he said heavily. "One of our agents, James Hartwell, vanished in Russia a little more than two months ago. We want you to find out if he's alive and where he is. You don't have to rescue him. With the new relationship between the two countries,* we can take the necessary steps once we know where he is."

"And?"

"Do you remember the name of Richard Sorge?"

"Yes," I said. "He was the head of the Russian Fourth Bureau during World War II. He was arrested in Japan and executed there."

He nodded. "We have reason to believe that he was never executed, but that he's still alive and still the head of the Fourth Bureau. If so, he is the most dangerous man in the country, even though he would now be in his seventies. Since we know quite a bit about him, it would be a big help if we

---

* This improved relationship may refer to the meeting of President Johnson and Premier Kosygin in June 1967, or the Soviet Union joining the U.S. and sixty other nations in signing the Non-Proliferation Treaty in July 1968, to avoid the spread of nuclear weapons. (However, that new relationship soured when the Soviet Union invaded Czechoslovakia in August 1968, around the time this book was being published.)

knew he was still alive and operating. We want you to check this out."

I looked at him. "If he is still alive, are you aware that he will be hidden somewhere in the Kremlin? That he will be so carefully concealed that it would take a hundred super-bloodhounds to sniff him out? And that it will be practically impossible for an industrial consultant to get within shouting distance of him?"

"Are you quite finished, Major?"

"Then," he said, "I can only tell you that checking out Sorge has top priority. It is an assignment."

TWO

That was quite an assignment, I thought. Go to Russia, where they had my picture and my fingerprints, and find a master spy who had supposedly died—had certainly vanished—more than twenty years ago.

"Thanks," I told the General dryly. "I guess I'll see you at the camp."

"I'll be there," he said. He gave me an equally dry smile and glanced toward the bedroom door. "Enjoy yourself, my boy." He picked up his briefcase and marched out of the suite.

Well, that was my boy. I'd known him for more than twenty years and he'd always been the same. I shrugged and went over to check the dresser. I had to admit that they did a good job. The identification was as complete as it was possible to be. I put everything in my pockets. The gun was as good as he'd said. I put it in my holster. Then I added the hotel key and the Chicago apartment keys to my pocket and went over to the bedroom. I tapped lightly and opened the door.

She was stretched out on the bed, wearing only a nightgown, which was the same as nothing. She was quite a sight. She had a glass of champagne in one hand and a cigarette in the other. She looked up and smiled.

"Business all finished?" she asked.

"Yes," I said. "Get dressed."

The smile faded from her face. "You mean you don't like me?"

"I don't mean anything of the kind. But you have been paid for the whole night, haven't you?"

"Yes."

"Have you had dinner?"

"No, but I had a late lunch."

"Well, I haven't had dinner either and I'm hungry. Right now, you and I are going out to dinner. The night is young."

Her smile returned. She slipped from the bed and pulled the nightgown over her head. It almost made me sorry that I had suggested dinner.

"I will be ready right away," she said. "Shall I come into the next room?"

"Sure," I said.

I went back to the living room and made myself a quick martini. I had barely finished it when she appeared. She was well dressed and, whore or not, looked chic enough to take anywhere. We went downstairs and stopped at the desk. I asked if I had any mail. The clerk handed me two envelopes. One had a stamp on it and the other didn't.

I opened the one without the stamp first. It was from the Soviet consulate and asked me if I would telephone at my convenience on a matter that had already been discussed with my State Department. I put it in my pocket and opened the other. It contained a check for one thousand dollars from the Brotherhood Coin Vending Company. A man named Benotti had signed it. I endorsed it and gave it to the clerk. I told him that they could cash it and give me the difference when I checked out. He gave me a receipt for the check.

"Let's go, honey," I said to the girl.

We went out and got a cab. I noticed that another cab pulled out right behind us, but then I forgot about it. We went to a club on the east side where I wasn't known and wouldn't be too apt to run into anyone who knew me.

We had a few drinks and dinner and watched the show and got acquainted. Contrary to what a lot of people might think, she turned out to be pretty intelligent and on the ball. I started to ask her about her interests.

She had just finished telling me about her collection of jazz records when she stopped suddenly. There was a funny little smile on her face as she looked at me. "I want to ask one favor," she said.

"Go ahead."

"You can ask me anything you want, but please don't ask me one question."

"Which one is that? I wasn't about to propose, if that's what you meant."

She laughed, but there was tension back of it. "I meant please don't ask me how a nice little girl like me got into a business like this."

"What business?" I asked. "Don't tell me that you're some kind of lady executive. I couldn't stand it. But I'll tell you what I'll do. I'll make a bargain with you."

"What?"

"I won't ask you that question if you promise not to ask me how a nice man like me got into the business I'm in."

She laughed. At first it sounded a little hysterical, but then it softened and was natural. "Do you mean," she asked, "because you're carrying a gun?"

"Now, now," I said, "we're making a bargain. You don't ask me about the gun and I won't ask you about the nightgown."

She laughed again. "Okay, Peter. Miloff is a Russian name, isn't it? Is that a safe question?"

"Yes twice."

"But you're an American."

I looked at her. "Don't suddenly get thick in the head," I said. "Yes, I am what is generally known as an American. I even have a birth certificate to prove it. I think, however, the only real Americans are Indians, but somewhere along the line a bunch of disgruntled Englishmen took the franchise away from them. Now all of us are Americans and they are our wards. We take care of them by making sure that they don't get their hands on the loot and get contaminated. We keep them simple and pure. It's a neat formula. We give them God's love; our own love we keep for more important things, such as a quick meeting in some dirty little motel. It keeps everything in its place."

She looked at me curiously. "I've known a few men who carried guns, but I never knew one who talked like that."

"I've known a few women who wore nightgowns, but they didn't talk like you. Besides, I thought we'd agreed that there was to be no conversation about guns or nightgowns."

"Sorry," she said.

The rest of the conversation was unimportant, but pleasant. We finally left the club at about two in the morning. We took a cab back to the hotel, followed dutifully by a second cab, and went up to the suite. I escorted her into the bedroom.

"It's all yours, honey," I said.

She looked at me strangely and then came over to me. "You're a strange man, Peter," she said. "But I like you."

She leaned up to kiss me. It started out as a friendly kiss, but something happened to it in transit. I never did make it to the couch where I had intended to sleep.

When I awakened the next morning, she was already up and dressing. "Hey," I said, "where are you going?"

"I thought I'd leave without waking you up," she said. "I'm sorry."

"Stay for breakfast. Then you can leave."

She hesitated. "All right," she said finally.

I went in and took a shower while she finished dressing. Then I dressed quickly. I led the way into the living room and went to the phone.

"What do you want for breakfast?" I asked her.

"Just orange juice, toast, and black coffee," she said.

"That's not enough for a growing girl," I protested.

"That's all," she said firmly. "I have to watch my weight"

"Nonsense," I said. "You could stand to gain a few pounds. How about a Bloody Mary?"

"All right," she said reluctantly.

I called room service and ordered her breakfast and ham and eggs for myself, plus a Bloody Mary and a double martini. I glanced at her. She still looked beautiful, which is difficult for anyone after so little sleep and so much to drink.

"You're lovely," I said.

She looked surprised. "Thank you, Peter. I think your eyesight must be slightly off this morning, but I appreciate it anyway."

We made some more small talk, and then the waiter arrived with our order. I signed the check, adding the tip, and he left. We made more small talk while we had breakfast.

"Now," she said when we had finished, "I must leave."

She came over and kissed me on the cheek. "Thank you for everything. Peter, You're from out of town, aren't you?"

I nodded.

"How long are you staying in town?"

"I think only two or three more days."

She looked embarrassed as she took a card from her purse and put it on the breakfast table. "If you feel like calling me while you're still in town, or when you come back, it will be, as they used to say in my father's bar, on the house."

"Thank you, honey," I said seriously. "And you can always reach me at the Brotherhood Coin Vending Company in Chicago—if you want anyone shot, it'll be on the house."

She threw back her head and laughed with a healthy sound. "I may do that," she said, "but I do hope you'll call, if only to say hello. Good-bye, Peter."

"Good-bye, Merry," I said, and watched her walk out. She had a nice walk.

I smoked a cigarette and finally picked up the phone book and found the number of the Russian consulate. I called them and asked for Mr. Kirilenko, the name that was signed to the letter I had received. I told them that Peter Miloff was calling.

It was only a minute before another voice came on. "Mr. Miloff?" he asked.

"Yes," I said. "I'm calling because you wrote me a letter—I presume you are Mr. Kirilenko?"

"Yes."

"You asked me to phone you, and that is what I am doing."

"I am grateful that you have done so," he said. His English was excellent, with only a slight accent. "Are you aware of the reason for my letter, Mr. Miloff?"

"Yes. I was told by my company that you would be in touch with me."

"Excellent, Mr. Miloff. Could you have lunch with me here today so that we can discuss it at length?"

"What time?"

"Say twelve-thirty."

"Yes, I think I could make that."

"Then I will expect you at twelve-thirty, Mr. Miloff."

There was a click as he hung up.

I called room service and asked them to send up some ice, a bottle of V.O., and a newspaper. The waiter arrived in a few minutes. I made myself a drink and read the paper. Then I went into the bathroom and shaved and got ready for my big luncheon date. I went downstairs, checked to see if there was any more mail, and then went out to get a taxi. I told the driver to take me to the Russian consulate. I ignored the look he gave me and we drove up Park Avenue in silence. I paid him off and entered the building on the corner.

I was expected. The receptionist immediately took me to a room on the third floor. There was a table already set up for lunch. Then I noticed the man sitting at the table. He was about my age, but his hair was already gray. He stood up as I looked at him and smiled.

"Vwi mozhetyeh govorit porusski?" he asked.

"Da, mogu," I said.

"Good," he said, continuing in the same language. "Our message from Moscow mentioned that you spoke our language, but it didn't say how well. Won't you sit down?"

"Spasibo," I said. I took the chair across from him, noticing that the table was set for just the two of us.

"I am Ivan Kirilenko," he said. "I know that your name is Peter Miloff. It is a Russian name, is it not?"

"Yes. My family came here about a hundred years ago."

"Ah, those were bad days," he said. "Comrade Mikoyan speaks very highly of your company, and your company speaks very highly of you. Will you have some vodka?"

"Thank you," I said again.

He poured and we both drank. "There are not many things to discuss, so we might as well complete our business before lunch. As you probably know, we asked your company to recommend a specialist who might be willing to work in Russia for a few months. They recommended you. We made a formal announcement of our intentions to your State Department, and they have informed us that they have no objection."

"I was told this by my company."

"Now we come to the matter of terms," he said, refilling our glasses. "We were told by your company that you are a highly paid specialist. We are willing to pay you your regular salary while you are in Russia. One thousand dollars per week. We will also furnish you with an apartment in Moscow and with all of your travel expenses. Is that satisfactory?"

"Yes."

He smiled at me. "I notice that you carry a gun. Is that customary in your profession?"

I returned his smile. "Sometimes it is necessary."

"Ah, yes, we've heard about your city of Chicago. I am afraid, however, that you will not be permitted to bring the gun into my country."

"That's all right. I probably won't need it there. I may need to bring some other things with me."

"Such as?"

Actually, I wasn't sure, but I thought I'd better prepare him. "I'll probably bring some plans for standard machines, and I imagine I'd better bring some special tools. I will also want to bring a tape recorder and a camera."

"We could furnish those."

"I prefer to use ones with which I am familiar." I smiled at him. "Your people can examine them as much as they wish. I am coming to your country as a specialist in vending machines, not as a spy."

He laughed. "I don't think there will be any objection to such things. When would you like to leave?"

"Well," I said, "I came to New York on business for my company. It will take me another two or three days to finish, then I will have to return to Chicago to report the results. I am then scheduled to go on a two-week vacation at a camp in Upstate New York, which is owned by my employer. I would like to take that vacation, since I imagine I'll be working pretty hard in the next few months."

"That is satisfactory," he said. "Shall we plan on you leaving in about three weeks?"

"That sounds about right."

"Good. I will arrange for your necessary Russian papers, including your contract." He raised his glass. "To a successful visit to our country."

We both drank and he refilled the glasses. "Now we will have lunch," he said.

I didn't see him press a button or make any other signal, but the doors opened and several waiters came in with the food. There was enough for seven or eight people, not to mention the vodka that he kept pouring. The proletariat never had it so good.

While we ate, and had more vodka, Kirilenko spoke of the things I might enjoy in Moscow. He made it sound inviting. We had brandy with the coffee and drank another toast to my mission in Russia.

I left shortly after lunch, promising that I would call him as soon as I returned from my vacation. I went straight back to the hotel, noticing that I was still being followed. That would probably continue until I took off in a Russian plane.

My biggest problem was to seem to be busy for a couple of days. I did go and make sure my passport was in order, but after that I was on my own—except that I was being followed by one or more Russians at all times. So I visited dealers in vending machines, posing as a possible buyer, and wandered around the city looking at cigarette machines, sandwich and coffee machines, pinball games, and anything else I could think of. The Russians dutifully followed me, and I pretended not to know they were there. On the third day I checked out of the hotel and went to Chicago.

Somebody else picked up my trail at O'Hare Airport as I took a cab to my Chicago address. It was a large, good-looking apartment building. It even had a doorman.

"Glad to have you back, Mr. Miloff," the doorman said as I got out of the cab.

I had to admit to myself that the Syndicate also had a good organization. I smiled at the doorman and tipped him. Then I went upstairs while he got someone to bring up my luggage.

It was a nice apartment, one that fitted the needs of a man who made a thousand dollars a week. I even thought that maybe I was in the wrong business. A man brought up my suitcases—the ones supplied by General Roberts—and I tipped him. As soon as he was gone, I checked through the apartment. There were five rooms, all furnished in excellent taste. The closets and the dressers were filled with clothes, all in my size and pretty much in my taste. I was sure that the shirts, for example, were new, but they had been laundered and there was nothing that would prove anything was brand new. There were even additional pieces of luggage, expensive but slightly worn. There was a well-equipped bar, with some of the bottles only partly full.

I took off my jacket and made myself a drink. Then I sat down and looked over my temporary domain. I liked it. I wondered if I could make a deal with Benotti to keep it after this was over. I got up and prowled around some more. They hadn't overlooked a thing. There were a couple of cartons of my brand of cigarettes. The liquor was all my kind. There was also a black phone book. Most of the names in it were of girls. I wondered what would happen if I started calling them.

Finally I picked up the phone and called the special number in Washington. General Roberts answered it himself.

"Well, if it isn't my Uncle Bobby," I said.

"Where are you?" he asked.

"In my apartment," I said. "Where else?"

"You know you're being followed?"

"You must be kidding," I said. "Nobody would follow little old me."

"Will you grow up?" he said in disgust. "We're leaving for the camp tonight. You'll be taken there tomorrow by the chauffeur—early in the morning. But first you have to stop in at the office and see your friendly employer, Mr. Benotti."

"Why?"

"He expects it. He wants a look at what he's recommended."

"That's nice. By the way, you did a nice job fixing up this apartment. What happens if I call any of the numbers in the phone book you left me?"

"You'll be talking to a girl," he said shortly. "She may cost you money if you want to do more than talk. But don't forget—early in the morning. We'll see you at the camp." He hung up.

Well, that was that. I had another drink and then decided to go out for dinner. I took a cab to the Palmer House, dutifully followed by my Russians. I had a fine dinner before going back to the apartment. I was tempted to call one of the numbers in the book just to see what would happen. My better sense finally triumphed, and instead I went through the apartment, packing things that I would want on a vacation. Then I had another drink and went to bed.

I was awakened by a ringing bell. At first I thought it was the telephone, but all I got when I'd picked it up was the dial tone. Finally I figured out that it was the house phone. I stumbled across to it and said hello.

"The chauffeur is here, Mr. Miloff," a voice said.

"All right," I groaned, "I'll be right down." I hung up and looked at my watch. It was six o'clock. What the hell, I wondered, were Syndicate people doing up at this hour? I took a quick shower, shaved, and got dressed. I was fully packed, so I just picked up the suitcase and went downstairs.

The car was a Cadillac and the chauffeur was correctly attired. But when you looked a little closer, you could see the bulge under his left arm, and his face was that of a hood.

"Mr. Miloff," he said, "Mr. Benotti is waiting to see you."

"Doesn't anybody in this town ever sleep?" I grumbled as I got into the back seat.

"We have a long drive ahead of us," he said with a smile, "and Mr. Benotti wanted to see you before we left."

"Okay," I said.

We drove out to an area where there was nothing but expensive houses and pulled into the driveway of one of them. The chauffeur parked right in front of the house.

"Mr. Benotti is waiting," he said.

I marched up to the front door and pushed the button. The door was opened by a butler, but he looked like a hood too. I told him my name and he led the way into a huge study. There was a big, fat man sitting behind the desk. He looked up as I came in.

"Miloff?" he said. "I'm Angelo Benotti." He held out a pudgy hand. I shook it. "Want some coffee? A drink?"

"Both," I said. "I'm not accustomed to being up at this hour."

He laughed. "Neither am I. Help yourself. The coffee is there and the booze over there."

I poured myself a cup of coffee and then took a big shot of brandy and went back to the chair in front of his desk. "To your good health," I said.

"Yours," he answered. "I'm sorry to bring you here at this hour, but you have a long drive ahead of you to reach the camp, and I thought I ought to see the guy I suggested for a job. I see you're smart enough to carry some hardware."

"Yeah," I said. "I don't like to go out in the snow barefoot."

He laughed. "That's smart. When you get back from that Commie country, you want a job, you look up Angelo Benotti. I like boys who go out and do something for their country."

"Thank you," I said humbly. "It's very good of you to let me use your apartment and your camp."

"It's nothing," he said with a wave of his hand. "This country has been good to me. Why shouldn't I be good to it?"

It took a little effort, but I managed to keep a straight face. "That's the way I feel, sir," I said. I downed the coffee and brandy.

"I'm glad to hear it," he said. "Well, I know you have to leave. Believe me, you can put complete trust in Roberto. He is a good man and knows this business from top to bottom."

"Roberto?" I asked.

"Ah," he said. "He didn't tell you his name. Roberto

Granetti. He is the one who is driving you and who will teach you about our machines. He is one of my best men. He is part of my family. You understand?"

"I understand." I started to leave, and got as far as the door.

"One more thing," Benotti said softly. "I am glad to do anything I can for my country. My country and my family are the same so far as I'm concerned. By helping to get you to Russia, I have in a way made you a member of the family. Do you also understand this?"

"Yes."

"Be sure to do a good job, Peter Miloff. My honor is at stake as much as yours is. Don't let me down. If you do, I will have to do something about it."

THREE

That had a familiar ring to it. Here was a man who was part of the biggest gang of thieves and murderers the world had ever known, but he had to try to prove he was a good American—so good that if I didn't do the job the way he thought I ought to, he'd deal out his own brand of justice.

"Don't worry about it," I told him with a smile. "If I don't do a good job, I won't be around for you to do anything about it."

"They play rough over there, huh?"

"They play so rough they have guys that would make some of your boys look like ping-pong players."

He frowned, then laughed. "Yeah, I guess maybe they're pretty good at it. Well, good luck."

I went out to the car. This time I started to get in the front seat with the chauffeur.

"Better sit in the back," he said. "We're being tailed and they might think it was funny if you're up front."

I got into the back and relaxed. He took off as I lit a cigarette.

"Push the button in front of you," he said. "It opens a bar with about anything in it you could like."

I pushed the button. He was right. The whole back of the seat swung out and there was a complete bar, including ice cubes. I poured some V.O. over ice.

"How about you?" I asked.

"Not now," he said.

I glanced over my shoulder once we threaded our way through traffic and spotted the car that was following us. There were two men in it.

"They ain't cops," Granetti said.

"Russians," I replied.

"Well, they'll get to look at some of the country."

Once we got outside of the Chicago city limits, I lost interest in the car tailing us. I had a couple of drinks, then stretched out on the back seat and went to sleep. I slept for almost three hours. When I awakened, I saw we were going through the countryside at a steady seventy miles an hour. I looked through the rear window. The comrades were still keeping up. I made myself a fresh drink.

"I see our little friends are still with us," I said.

"Yeah," Granetti grunted. "I ain't tried to lose them. I figured maybe you wouldn't want that."

"Right. Let them have their fun. If we lost them, they'd only start to sulk and decide it was a funny way for a guy to act when he's on a vacation."

We drove on for a couple more hours and then pulled up to a roadside stop. We left the car to be filled with gas and went inside the restaurant. It was pretty good, with tables as well as a food counter and a bar. We took a table. Granetti had bourbon and I ordered a martini. While we were having our drinks I saw a man come in who looked like a Russian security agent. He bought some sandwiches and drinks at the food bar and left.

"I think that was one of our friends," I told Granetti. "He

took food out—so they don't chance our driving off while they're in the middle of a meal."

He grinned. "It's too bad we can't lose them. We could outrun that heap they're in and it wouldn't take more'n ten minutes."

I shrugged. "It wouldn't do anything except make them suspicious, and they probably know where the camp is anyway."

"Yeah." He looked at me curiously. "I guess you'll soon be tailed by a lot of them, huh?"

"You know where I'm going?"

"Yeah. The boss told me, but don't worry. I button up about everything."

"I imagine there'll be a few of them around most of the time," I said dryly.

He was still staring at me. "You some kind of cop?" he asked.

I smiled. "I suppose some people might call me that, but I'm sure a cop wouldn't. Actually, I'm in the United States Army."

"Yeah? I got a kid in the Army. He's in Vietnam right now."

For just a minute I was surprised. It's hard to realize sometimes that people like that have kids just like the rest of us and that they grow up to do most of the same things other kids do.

"How does he like it?" I asked.

"What's to like? At least, I'd rather have him ducking bullets there than ducking some of the ones here." He looked at my left shoulder. "You wear that like a pro."

"I am a pro," I told him gently. I thought I might as well get that part of it settled at once. "You know the business I'm in and I know the business you're in. But don't sell my business short on that score. There are more notches on this gun than you'll ever have on yours, and none of them were made on a battlefield. As a matter of fact, I've never been on what the Army calls a battlefield."

He continued to stare at me for a minute, then laughed. "I'll have to write my son about this. He'll get a kick out of it."

"Just be careful what you write."

"Don't worry," he said quickly. "I told you I know how to button up. I won't tell him anything that will hurt what you're doing. You ever meet the boss before?"

"No."

"He's smart, the boss. He told me you were a tough baby and not to get any ideas."

"When did he tell you that?"

"While you were coming out of the house. He's got a direct radio contact to the phone in the car."

"Okay," I said. "If it helps any, I know that he's a tough baby, too—and so are you. Now, are we all squared away? We understand each other?"

"Sure," he said.

We had our lunch and started driving again. The other car dutifully followed us when we pulled away from the road-side place.

I mixed myself another drink from the bar and relaxed. We hit seventy miles an hour again and held it.

The sun was just setting as we hit Plattsburg, New York. "It's about two miles from here," Granetti said as we turned into a narrow road.

The other car followed us until we finally pulled off into a private driveway. Then it went on past as if it had no interest in us.

"Where do you think they're going?" he asked.

"Probably to a motel in Plattsburg. Then they'll come back and keep watch. One of them on land with binoculars, I would guess, and the other on the lake."

He drove in and stopped in front of the garage. Maybe they called this place a camp, but in my circles it would have been a mansion. The main house looked as if it had about twenty rooms. The garage had enough room for six cars, and there was an apartment above it. The buildings were surrounded by trees, and beyond them I could see the large lake.

We both got out of the car and stretched. It had been a long ride.

"Want me to help you with your luggage?" he asked.

"Are you kidding?" I asked. "I have one suitcase. If I can't carry that, I'd better retire."

"I think your friends are already in the house. But the brass key on the ring you picked up for the apartment fits the door of the house."

"What are you going to do?" I asked.

He pointed to the garage. "I have an apartment up there."

"How about dinner? I don't know the situation, but why don't you come over to the house?"

"Thanks," he said, "but I have everything in the apartment. I think you'll find everything in the main house you'll need, although you'll have to do your own cooking. If you want me for anything, there's a direct phone."

"Okay," I said, and pulled my suitcase out of the car.

"We'll start to work on the machines tomorrow," he said. "But there's one thing I should tell you."

"What?"

"Don't go out of the house after dark. If you want to, call me and I'll come and get you."

"Why?"

"As soon as it's dark there'll be two Dobermans running around the grounds. They know me, but they won't know you. I wouldn't want to see you hurt and I wouldn't want one of them killed."

"Does that go on all the time?"

"Yes."

"Then you must have a caretaker?"

"Yes," he said again. He pointed through the trees to the left. There was a small building visible there. "He lives there all the time. He takes care of the dogs and turns them loose every night as soon as it's dark. They come in again at daylight. They're good dogs, but they're not very friendly."

"Thanks for telling me," I said. "That means that I'm practically a prisoner here."

"No. If you want to go out—and maybe you should, since you're supposed to be on vacation—just call me, and I'll come and get you. If you want a broad, let me know. There are several in the neighborhood. I'll go pick them up. That's about the only kind of action there is around here."

"Maybe I should go out one or two nights," I said. "Now for something else. We can be fairly certain that we're going to be watched constantly. I'm going out to fish every morning and will spend some time just sitting out in the sun. We'll do our work after that. Can we do any shooting around here?"

"Yeah. There are some targets in the woods. The background is the lake, so it's safe."

"I suggest then that we do a little shooting each day in the middle of working on the machines."

"Smart," he said. "Come over whenever you're ready tomorrow."

"Okay. Thanks."

I picked up my suitcase and went over to the house. I used the key to open the front door and went in. It was quite a house. I wandered through it until I came to something that looked like a combination playroom and study. The draperies were all drawn, so it was a little dark. I flicked on a light and there they were—General Sam Roberts and two men I didn't know. All three of them had drinks in their hands.

"Well," I said, "I'm glad to see that everyone has made himself at home. Drinking high on the crime octopus. But there's no light in the window for the wayfarer."

"We were invited to make use of the supplies here," General Roberts said stiffly. "Martin Haywood and Eddie Mays, Peter Miloff. He is a very good man in the field, but completely impossible otherwise. However, he's our man for the job."

I shook hands with the two men. Haywood was a big, hulking man, wearing a tweed suit and looking like a professor. Mays was short and slight, with blond hair and the look of a thief.

"Pay no attention to the General," I told them. "He can't get over the fact that I knew him when he was a chicken colonel. How come no lights?"

"We thought," General Roberts said, "that we shouldn't have any lights until you arrived, in case your little friends were watching."

"Good thinking," I said ironically. "Two of them followed us all the way from Chicago. I imagine they are now getting a motel room in Plattsburg. They'll be watching us, I believe, from both sea and land every day." I paused. "How's the food supply?"

"Great," Mays said. "There's probably more stuff in the freezer than the Waldorf has."

"I gather," I said, "that there's enough in the way of booze, too."

"We arrived here before daylight this morning," General Roberts said formally, "and this is the first drink we've had."

"Bully for you," I said. "Let's not be so moral about the whole thing. Mr. Benotti is anxious to prove that he's a good American instead of a plain hood. Drink his booze and eat his food. You've already paid for it. Now, who's going to do the cooking around here?"

"I'm a fairly good cook," Haywood said. "I'll be glad to prepare meals."

"Good," I said. "It's been a long day and I'm hungry. What's the setup here so far as my two weeks are concerned?"

"Mr. Haywood," General Roberts said, "will brief you on the assignment. Mr. Mays will brief you on certain methods to be used."

"What are you going to do?" I asked, "I mean aside from flashing the brass on your shoulders."

His face had turned almost purple. "March," he said, "I'm

going to bring you up on charges if you continue to talk like this."

"Really? You forget that this time I'm a civilian volunteer and not a member of the armed forces. Therefore I am not subject to a court martial. And, with all due respect to your position, General, I'm the one who is making the trip, so I will make the final decisions on everything. Is that clear?"

"Yes," he said, but he sounded as if he were about to strangle.

"One more thing. My name is Peter Miloff, and I am not to be called March under any circumstances or you may blow the whole thing. You may have already. Too many people are interested in a guy named March."

The color had vanished from his face. "You're right, Peter," he said. "I'm sorry. I got so angry I forgot."

"I'm not rubbing it in, General," I said, "but this is a must. It might even be too late. There may be some communication between here and the garage. If there is, we'll know in a day or so. Now, there's one more thing I have to say. No one is to step outside of this house while it's dark."

"Why?" Haywood asked.

"The minute it gets dark there are two Dobermans roaming the grounds. I gather that they are not friendly. And of course, none of you is to go outdoors or show yourself at a window during the day. Is this clear?"

All three of them nodded.

"Okay. Martin, will you see what you can scare up to eat? Where's the booze?"

Haywood smiled as he got up. "Right over there. You can't miss it."

I looked in the direction he was pointing and he was right. There was a bar big enough to be in a joint on Broadway. Haywood left the room and I went over to the bar and made myself a martini. I took off my jacket and sprawled out in a chair.

"How are the sleeping arrangements?" I asked.

"There are five bedrooms," the General said. He gave me his ironic smile. "We have saved the master bedroom for you."

"Touching," I said. "We who are about to die salute you for your concern. I get a hearty meal and a comfortable bed—both by courtesy of the Syndicate—before I go out to do or die. Of course, you get the same hearty meal and comfortable bed—from the same source—but then all you have to do is go man the front desk. I guess that's the way one becomes a general. I've often wondered."

Eddie Mays was enjoying it, but trying not to show it. General Roberts was beginning to get a little red in the face again.

"Forget it," I said. I got up and mixed another martini. "Have a drink, General, before your blood pressure takes off without benefit of wings. I just have one more thing to say and then we'll all relax and have a restful evening at home."

I waited while he and Eddie Mays poured themselves drinks. "We have to remember that as far as our Russian friends are concerned, I am on a well-earned vacation. There are going to have to be some signs of relaxation. So I'm going to do a little swimming, a little fishing, some shooting with Granetti, and I might even go into town one or two nights. In between, we will work and do a certain amount of quiet drinking and eating. We have two weeks, so we don't have to rush too much."

Martin Haywood came in to refresh his drink. "Boy," he said, "is that a kitchen! If there's anything he doesn't have in there, it hasn't been grown or invented yet."

"The result of honest toil," I said lightly. "What are we having tonight?"

He filled his glass. "Well," he said, "the meat and fowl are all frozen, so there isn't enough time to thaw things out and then get together something ambitious. I thought we'd have steak tonight. We'll get a little fancier as time goes on."

"Sounds good enough," I said.

He went back to the kitchen.

I got up and wandered around the room. It was difficult to think of it as a room since it was roughly the size of a large apartment. I found the color television and turned it on. Then, carrying my martini, I continued to look around. There were a couple of radios, a stereo set, and I finally discovered a hidden screen and, beyond one of the walls, a projection room and reels of maybe a hundred movies. All the comforts of home.

There was also a pool table and several slot machines, By trying them, I discovered that the slot machines paid out real money when you hit. I went over to the pool table and racked up the balls. Eddie Mays's face lit up as he came over. General Roberts stared grumpily at us while we played a few games. I had another martini and Eddie had another bourbon.

Haywood stuck his head in. "How do you like your steaks?"

"Rare," Eddie Mays and I both said. The General said he

liked his medium rare, and Haywood vanished again. It wasn't much longer before we were called to dinner.

I had to admit that Haywood had done a good job. The steaks were charcoal-broiled to perfection, and there were baked potatoes, mixed vegetables with a cheese sauce over them, a fine salad, and a bottle of good red wine.

I took a bite of the steak. It was great. "My compliments to the chef," I said to Haywood. "I didn't know this was a talent we cultivated in our department."

"It's really only a hobby," Haywood said.

"Haywood was a professor at Harvard," General Roberts said.

"It only proves the advantages of higher education," I replied, winking at Haywood.

We had coffee in the study. I had brandy with mine, then went into the projection room and picked out a recent movie and put it on the projector. I went back to the study, turned off the TV set, and pushed the button that revealed the screen. Then I headed for the projector again, but on my way back I detoured via the front door. I looked through the window to one side. There was a light over the front of the garage, but that was the only outside light. I thought I saw a scurrying object on the lawn, so I opened the door.

I'd been right. Within two seconds there was a big, sleek black dog ten feet away. He was staring at me with his tongue hanging out. Something about his expression reminded me of the way I felt when I had looked at my steak at dinner.

FOUR

The dog had convinced me. I closed the door and went back to the study to start the movie. It was good, but I was tired. I had another brandy and decided I was through for the day.

"Where is this so-called master bedroom?" I asked.

"Upstairs," General Roberts said, "first door to the right."

"I'll leave the hall light on, I said. "Watch about any lights in the other bedrooms. I'll see you tomorrow." I picked up my suitcase and went upstairs.

The master bedroom also looked about the size of a whole apartment. The bed was a round one, at least eight feet in diameter. I didn't waste too much time admiring it. I unpacked my suitcase and put things away. Then I got into bed. I was asleep almost the minute I put my head on the pillow.

I was up at five in the morning. I made some coffee and smoked a cigarette while I drank it. Then I put on a pair of trunks and went out for a swim. When I got back I sat on the patio for about an hour. The sun was good and hot. Finally, I went upstairs, showered and shaved, and got dressed. By the time I came back down, the others were up and having breakfast. I had a drink at the bar and then made some bacon and eggs for myself.

"Good morning," I said cheerfully as I joined them in the dining area.

They all said good morning, and Haywood asked me, "Have a nice swim?"

"Great," I said. "There's a little man out there in a boat pretending to fish. He also has a lovely pair of binoculars— probably so he can see the fish better."

"What's next on the agenda?" the General asked.

"I'm going to have my breakfast, then I think I'll go fishing. We can have the catch for lunch."

After breakfast and another drink, I took a couple of cans of beer from the refrigerator, picked up an opener, and went out to the boathouse. I found fishing equipment and loaded everything into a rowboat. There was a power boat, which I ignored. I rowed out into the lake. The little man was still there, but I paid no attention to him. I opened a can of beer and started fishing.

Two good-sized trout later, I decided to call it a day. I rowed back to the boathouse and cleaned the fish. Then I went up to the house and turned my catch over to Haywood. He agreed to fix the fish for lunch.

It was still a little early to call Granetti, so I made a big drink, found a book, and went out on the patio again. I figured I might as well let the man in the rowboat get a good look at a vacationing capitalist. I stayed out there until almost noon and then went inside and smelled the cooking from the kitchen. I was glad that someone in the agency had more than one talent.

I mixed a martini and looked at the phone on the bar. There was an intercom button. I lifted the receiver and pushed the button.

"Yeah," Granetti said.

"When do you want me to come over?"

"Make it in a couple of hours if that's all right," he said. "I just got up and I thought I'd take a swim and then have some breakfast."

"A couple of hours is fine. See you then." I put the receiver down and went over to sit in the big chair. General Roberts gave me a sour look.

"You should be working," he said.

"I'm a man on vacation," I said with a smile. "That guy out in the boat—we don't want to spoil his illusions about decadent capitalists."

He grunted as I went over to make another martini. I had just finished it when Haywood announced that lunch was ready.

The trout was great.

"There's still some time before I have to go to the garage," I said when we'd finished coffee. "General, why don't you do the dishes while I put in a little work with the boys?"

He didn't like the suggestion, but he could hardly complain since he'd just been grumbling about me not getting to work. Haywood and Mays followed me back into the study. I made myself a drink and looked at them. They were both grinning as they listened to the sounds from the kitchen.

"Which one of you is going to brief me on what?" I asked. "As usual, the General neglected to mention little things like that."

"Martin is going to brief you on the assignment," Eddie Mays said. I'm the gimmick man."

"Good enough," I said. "Martin, why don't you give me the overall picture of the assignment and then you can go into detail during the next two weeks."

"Right," he said.

He went over to the bar and made himself a bourbon and soda. Then he sat down, filled his pipe, and lit it. "There are two jobs, actually, although they may be related. There is also the problem of handling everything extra carefully."

"I like staying alive, so I'll do that anyway."

"I don't mean just for that reason. I'm sure you're aware of the present tensions between Russia and China. This has, in turn, pushed the Russians into a somewhat friendlier position in relation to us. We don't want to do anything to disturb this new balance, if possible."

"Okay. So I'm also a diplomat."

"The first part of the assignment," Martin said carefully, "is to try to locate one of our agents. His name is James Hartwell. The records don't show that you ever met him. He's one of our best agents. James vanished somewhere in Russia almost three months ago. He may be dead, but we don't think so. We believe that he's in a Russian prison somewhere, yet we haven't been able to get even a hint. They are probably working on him to make him talk."

"Will he?"

He shook his head. "I don't think so. He's been worked over before and never talked. But if he's alive, we want him found."

"And then what?"

"Well, it would be nice if you shipped him back to us," he

said with a smile, "but I don't suppose the Russians will cooperate. Actually, kidnapping him to get him out might present other problems at this particular time. But if you can find where he is, then we might be able to open negotiations to exchange one of their men for him. So far, however, the Russians have refused to admit that they've ever heard of James Hartwell. Other undercover agents have failed to learn anything."

"Where was he when you last heard from him?"

"Moscow. Now, your other assignment is to finish the job he was on."

"Which is?"

"Did you ever hear of the Fourth Bureau?"

I remembered what General Roberts had said. "Yes. It was a branch of Red Army Intelligence before and during World War II."

"Right. Now, what do you know about a man named Richard Sorge?"

"He was a Russian spy who operated in Japan. He was supposedly arrested there and executed."

"Well," he said, "that's part of the problem. Richard Sorge was the head of the Fourth Bureau and was probably the most successful spy the Russians ever had. He was arrested and was supposed to be executed. We're not so sure he was."

"Why?"

"We think a deal was made. There are several things that would seem to substantiate this. There was an unusually long period of time between his conviction and the announcement of his execution. During that period Sorge had extensive dental work done in the prison and he also bought some new clothes—a little strange for a man who expects to die. The only witnesses at the execution were Japanese—also unusual in the case of the execution of a non-national."

"Interesting," I said.

"That isn't quite all. Sorge was betrayed to the Japanese by a girl. A short time later she was murdered. In the next couple of years, several people swore that they saw Sorge in China. Then nothing more was heard about him, but we believe that he's still alive and still active."

"He'd be about seventy now, wouldn't he?"

"Early seventies. Now, the Fourth Bureau was supposedly done away with shortly after World War II, but we think that it has continued to operate as an independent and small super-spy agency with special agents assigned to it from Red Army Intelligence and KGB, and that Richard Sorge has been and is the director of it. But this is only a theory. Personally, I believe it to be true. There is, however, not one scrap of real evidence."

"That's what Hartwell was working on?"

He nodded. "He must have gotten very close to the truth, too. Hartwell was a real pro."

"Sure," I said, "but he got caught. Do you have any leads?"

"No leads."

"That's quite a job," I said dryly. "And I'm supposed to do this while I'm showing the Russians how to build slot machines?"

"It's a perfect cover since they asked for you, and you should have more freedom than might normally be expected. And we can also give you some help."

"What kind?"

"We have four people inside Russia who have been working for us for a long period of time. Hartwell worked with them. Two are Russian nationals and two are Yugoslavs."

"Hartwell worked with them, and he vanished."

"I suppose it's possible that one of them betrayed him," Martin said, "but we're inclined to doubt it. Naturally, you can use your own judgment once you're on the scene."

"I intend to," I said flatly. "Who are the four people?"

"Grigory Masinov. He is a member of KGB, and we intend to instruct him to try to be assigned to you when you reach Russia. He has worked for us for four years and has always been reliable. His code name is Tolstoy."

"Ooh, somebody's been reading," I said. "Who else?"

"Irina Simonova. She is a reporter for *Pravda*. She has worked for us for three years and has also been reliable. Her code name is Masha."

"Is she young and pretty?"

"I wouldn't know. She has been efficient. Then there is Josip Voukelitch. He is a Yugoslavian journalist assigned to Moscow. He is also an agent for Tito, but he has worked for us for two years. Has an excellent record."

I grunted and made myself another drink.

"The fourth one is Marya Rijekta, who is employed in the Yugoslavian embassy in Moscow. She is also an agent for Tito, but has worked for us for two years."

"Young and pretty?"

This time he smiled. "I have no way of knowing."

"But she's efficient?"

"Yes."

"I suppose that the last two also have code names?"

"Yes. Voukelitch's is Raskolnikov, and Rijekta's is Orloff's Wife. Your code name is Uncle Vanya."

"Thanks a lot," I interrupted.*

"Hartwell's code name was Nikita. We will provide you with drops where you can leave and receive messages. While we're here I'll give you everything we have on these four people and on Hartwell. That will include photographs, which you can memorize. I guess it's time now for you to go learn how to build a slot machine."

"Yeah," I said.

I finished my drink and went upstairs, put on my shoulder holster, and put the gun in it. Then I took a box of bullets and slipped them in my pocket. I went out and walked over to the garage. There was a button beside the door to the apartment. I pushed it and waited. Granetti came down in a couple of minutes. He looked at the gun, which was in plain view, since I wasn't wearing a jacket.

"Expecting trouble?" he asked.

"No. I thought if we finished in time we might try the targets you mentioned."

"Okay," he said.

He took a key from his pocket and unlocked the garage door, and we went inside.

The car was there, but so were about fifteen or twenty vending machines. I looked at them and felt dizzy.

---

* Milo is not thrilled with having as his code name the title character of Chekhov's play *Uncle Vanya*, who is a depressed, discontented loser. Raskolnikov is the main character in *Crime and Punishment*, a novel by Dostoevsky. *Orloff and His Wife* is a classic book of stories by Maksim Gorky.

"You mean I have to learn everything about all of those?" I asked.

"Yeah, but it'll be a breeze. There are blueprints here for each one of these, and you can take them with you. But in the meantime you are going to take each one of these machines apart—and I mean every single screw—and then put them back together again. By the time we've finished, you'll know how to build one out of the parts in a junkyard. Okay?"

"I guess it has to be, " I said. "Let's get started."

I hadn't worked so hard in years. For the next three hours I worked on machines, not only worked with my hands, but tried to memorize everything I was doing.

"Let's knock it off," Granetti said finally. "You're doing great. Think you remember everything you've done today?"

"I think so," I said.

He showed me a washroom in the back of the garage and I started getting rid of the grease.

"I'll wash upstairs," he said, "and get my gun. Then we'll try the targets."

He left, and I continued to get cleaned up. Then I went outside and looked around while I waited for him. There was a car parked down the road, almost concealed by the trees. I had an idea that the other Russian was there.

Granetti came downstairs, carrying a gun in his hand. We walked into the woods where the targets were.

"Be my guest," he said.

I fired one clip rapidly. I knew they were hitting all right, but when I was finished, he walked down to look at the target. There was a thoughtful expression on his face as he came back.

"Pretty damn good," he said. He was impressed, which was what I had intended.

He fired a round and did fairly well, but he did miss a few shots. Then we fired several rounds. He didn't do any better and I didn't do any worse.

"I guess you know how to use that," he said as we walked back to the garage.

"I ought to," I told him, "I've had enough practice. Do you feel like going into town tonight while I make like a man on a vacation?"

"Sure," he said. "What time?"

"What's the swinging time around here?" I asked.

He grinned. "I'd say about nine."

"Okay. Let me know when you're ready."

I went on into the main house and up to my room. I cleaned my gun, then took a shower and changed clothes before going downstairs. There was a cooking smell from the kitchen, and General Roberts and Eddie Mays were watching television. I made myself a martini and sat down to join them.

"What was the shooting about?" the General asked.

"Target practice," I said, smiling. "It fits the role. Two gangsters out in the country have to keep in form."

He wasn't amused, but he didn't say anything.

"I'm going out tonight after dinner," I said a minute later.

"What?" the General said. He sounded startled. "For what reason?"

"Our cover story," I said gently. "As far as the Russians know, I'm a swinging man on a vacation. I can't be expected to spend all of my time fishing or mucking around in the garage. Granetti is going to drive me in to visit the local sin spots."

He grunted. "I suppose," he said reluctantly, "it's a good idea, since they're watching you. But don't forget you still have a lot of work to do."

"How can I forget as long as you're around to remind me?" I got up to mix another martini. Then we watched the news without talking until dinner was ready.

"What's it like in the great big outdoors?" Eddie Mays asked while we were eating. "I feel like I'm going stir crazy in here."

"It's the same way out there," I told him. "The Russians are breathing down my neck on one side and the Mafia on the other. The General's good friend and the great American patriot Angelo Benotti gently reminded me that his honor was in my hands when I went to Russia and I'd better take good care of it."

"What did you tell him?"

"I reminded him that the Russians were also worried about their honor, so that if my trip was unsuccessful, there wouldn't be anybody around for him to punish for his loss of honor. It obviously hadn't occurred to him, and we parted on a gentle note."

The General was grumbling to himself, so the conversation more or less ground to a halt. I congratulated Haywood on his dinner when we'd finished. Then we went back to the study for coffee. I had brandy with mine.

It was almost time for Granetti and me to leave. I went upstairs and got ready. This included strapping on the holster and putting the gun into it. I went back downstairs to wait until nine.

General Roberts took one look at me. "If you're going on the town," he said, "why are you taking the gun?"

"I'm a method actor," I told him. "The Russians think I'm part of the Mob, so I have to be fully dressed or they might think I am inefficient."

"Just remember," he said coldly, "that Peter Miloff does not have a permit to carry a gun."

"I know," I said. "Can you imagine what a flap that would make in Washington if the state cops picked me up for carrying a gun? Somebody would have to pull some strings."

"Someday," he said darkly, "you're going to go too far."

The phone rang, interrupting our little chat. I glanced at it. The intercom button was lit up. I pushed it and picked up the receiver.

"Yeah?" I said.

"You ready?" Granetti asked.

"Sure."

"I'll meet you in front," he said, and hung up.

"Okay," I said to the three of them. "I'm off for fun and games. Enjoy television and don't forget that there's a whole room full of movie films. And keep the fights down low. I'll see you around."

I went to the front door and opened it. I didn't see Granetti, but I thought I heard a door closing. I stepped outside and pulled the door shut behind me.

The only light was the one over the garage. There was no sound, except the small insect life in the woods. I took one step and waited. I saw him right away, the big, sleek black dog. He wasn't in a hurry; he was just walking toward me with easy strides. I took out my gun and clicked the safety off.

FIVE

That was all I needed. I knew damn well it was a setup, but I wasn't going to sit by and let a Doberman have an evening snack from me. I held the gun loosely and watched the dog move. I intended to wait until he made the first leap.

"Lance," a voice called. It belonged to Granetti. I'd figured that, too. I was sure he was somewhere, watching.

The dog hesitated and looked toward the garage.

"Come here, Lance," the voice said, and Granetti stepped out into the light. The dog turned and padded off toward him. "You can come on now, Miloff."

"Thanks," I said.

I walked toward the garage, but I still kept the gun in my hand.

In the meantime he had opened the garage door. He was petting the dog on the head when I reached them. I walked past them and got into the front seat of the Cadillac. Then I put the gun away. A moment later he slid in beside me and started the motor.

"You almost lost a dog," I told him.

"I know," he said. He chuckled. "I was wondering which would upset Mr. Benotti the most, losing a dog or losing a guest. I figured out that it would bother him more to lose the dog."

"I was way ahead of you. I would have hated to make Mr. Benotti unhappy, but I would have hated even more to be unhappy myself."

He chuckled again as he started the car. "Well, it worked out all right," he said.

"This time," I answered. "If there is a next time, I may not wait so long."

He said nothing as he backed the car out, turned it around, and headed out of the driveway. We drove about a mile down the road before the car showed up behind us.

"There's a place on the edge of town where there's a lot of action," Granetti said. "I figured that's where we'd go, unless you've got a better idea."

"That's okay with me."

"Now I'd like to make a suggestion."

"Go ahead."

"That's one of the Commies behind us? Right?"

"It's a good guess."

"When we go into this joint," he said, "you get a table and I'll go to the bar."

"Why?"

"They got to know that I'm supposed to be Mr. Benotti's chauffeur," he said. "They know that I drove you to the camp. They think that you're part of Mr. Benotti's operation on a pretty high level. So they're going to think it funny if you and me sit together. They'll make more out of it than anybody in this country would. So it's better if we don't sit together. They ain't dummies, and you can bet they check up on such things."

"What if we both find a couple of broads we want to take home?"

He smiled. "Then you can be generous. You can let me and my broad drive you and your broad to wherever you're going, and then I come back and pick you up later. I think they'll go for that."

"You're probably right," I said. "I think it's a little silly, but we'll play it your way—unless it goes wrong."

"Right," he said.

We reached the edge of the city and turned into the parking lot of a restaurant and bar. The neon signs were bright and flashing. We parked and went inside. There were already about thirty people in the place, and the jukebox was blaring. Granetti stopped at the bar, and I went on and got a table. I ordered V.O. on the rocks.

People kept coming in. Most of them were couples, but there were some single women and men. One of the latter was the Russian I'd seen in the boat on the lake. He took a table not too far from me, but made a point of not looking at me.

I noticed that there was already a blonde sitting with Granetti, and I assumed that she was someone he knew from previous visits. There were several attractive women in the place, but I had already decided which one I liked the best. She was the cocktail waitress. She was small and dark, built like a brick house. I noticed that she fielded most of the passes that were made.

I went to work on it, but it was at least two hours before I even got a flicker. Another hour and she was starting to get friendly. Another hour and she was even more friendly.

I already knew her name. "When do you get off, Carol?" I asked as she brought me another drink.

"Why?" she countered. "I'm not interested in any of the motels around here, if that's what you're suggesting."

"I'm not suggesting anything," I said. "I have a car and a driver, and I thought maybe I could drop you off at your home."

"I have a roommate. You'd have to drop her off too."

"Where is she?"

"She's the blonde at the bar, the one talking to the big guy."

I laughed. "That makes it even easier. The big guy is my driver."

"We'll see," she said as she hurried off to wait on another table.

Later I saw her signal to the blonde, and the two of them went off in the direction of the ladies' room.

"Okay," she said when she brought me my next drink. "You can drive us home. I get off in an hour."

Within that time the restaurant began to clear out, although the bar business was going strong. Granetti and the blonde got up and left the bar. He winked at me as he went. A few minutes later Carol came out of the back. She had changed from her uniform to a dress. I stood up as she neared the table. As we went outside to the car, I saw the Russian hurrying to pay his bill.

Granetti and the blonde were already in the Cadillac. Carol and I got in the back seat and I was introduced to the blonde. Her name was Connie, and Granetti did know her from other visits.

The two girls turned out to have a small house in the country not far from the restaurant. The Russian dutifully followed us there.

"We might," Carol said when we stopped in front of the house, "invite you in for a drink, but I don't think we have anything except a couple cans of beer."

"That's easily solved," I said. I leaned forward and pressed the button on the back of the seat and the bar swung open. "We're both Boy Scouts. Take your pick." She laughed and reached over to grab two bottles.

"I guess we're stuck. Come on."

It was late when we finally left the house and drove back to the camp. The other car was still with us, but I imagine the Russian was beginning to get a little tired. Granetti walked with me to the front door of the main house while the two dogs looked on from a distance. I went straight upstairs and to bed.

I was up early the next morning, despite the hour we'd gotten home, and went out for a quick swim. The Russian was there in his rowboat. I didn't stay long. Back in the house, I made myself a martini. I had a second one while preparing ham and eggs for myself. The others began coming down in the middle of breakfast.

The first one down was Eddie Mays. "You're up early," he said.

"It's an old family recipe," I told him. "Early to bed and early to rise makes a man hungover and unwise."

He laughed and poured himself some coffee. "How were the sin spots?"

"Sinful."

"What's the schedule for today?" he asked, bringing his coffee to the table.

"I'm going fishing after breakfast," I said. "There's a tired Russian out on the lake, and I wouldn't want him to think he's wasting his time or money. Then I'll come back and spend some time with you, and this afternoon I'll work on vending machines again."

He sighed. "Well, at least you'll be busy. This place is beginning to bug me. If you happen to run into town, would you bring back some paperback books and newspapers?"

"Sure."

I finished my breakfast and went fishing, taking along some beer. I stayed out for a couple of hours, and this time I caught two trout and a good-sized bass. I took them back and cleaned them and delivered them to Haywood. After a shower and some fresh clothes, I told Eddie I was ready. The General was watching television, so we went into what must have been called the playroom. It had a pool table, a poker table, several slot machines, and its own bar.

I poured myself a drink. "I'm ready," I said.

"I don't really have to give you a lot," he said, "but I do have some gadgets you can take with you, and they might come in handy."

"Such as?"

"You'll get a small tape recorder. It's a logical thing for you to take with you so you can tape suggestions. This one will have a concealed switch. If you use it, you can record on one track, and there is only one machine in the world—in Washington—that will pick up what is recorded there. You can send such tapes out of Russia via the drop we've arranged."

"Gee," I said, "just like 007. Anything else?"

"The camera will also have a special switch. A camera is also logical and it will take regular film. But it has a second lens and a place for a roll of microfilm. I'm certain that both the tape recorder and the camera will pass any inspection they give it. I have models here, which I'll show you. But when you go back to Chicago, go to Fenner's store and buy a camera and a tape recorder. You'll be recognized, and the special ones will be given to you."

"That's all?"

"No. I suggest three other things. Some special cigarettes, mixed in with the ones you'd normally smoke, which will flare up enough when lit for you to take a picture in the dark. After that first flare, they will smoke normally. A fountain pen which works but which will also contain an electronic sweep that will enable you to spot any listening device. And a pair of glasses with very sensitive microphones built into the frames. They'll pick up any conversation between a hundred and a hundred and fifty feet."

I shook my head. "The other things might pass, but I doubt if the glasses would. Leave them out."

"Okay."

"And you're forgetting something else I want."

"What?

"Some kind of gun."

"No. We decided it would be too dangerous for you to try to bring one in. If you think you need one, buy it on the black market in Moscow."

He went upstairs and brought down a tape recorder and camera and showed me how they worked. I had to admit they were clever gimmicks and would probably pass the inspection they would be given as I entered Russia.

A little later we had lunch, and then I called Granetti on the intercom. "When do you want me to come over?" I asked him.

"In an hour or so," he said.

"Think you might feel like driving me into town sometime today? I want to pick up some cigarettes and newspapers."

"Why don't you take the car yourself? I'll leave the keys in it. Then I'll be ready to work by the time you get back."

"Okay," I said.

I had a drink, then went out to the garage. The door was open and the keys were in the Cadillac. I got in and drove away. I didn't get far before a car appeared in my rearview mirror.

I drove straight into Plattsburg and stopped at a little bookstore and tobacco shop. I got several newspapers and a handful of paperbacks for Eddie, and a carton of cigarettes for myself. Then I got into the Cadillac and returned to the camp with the other car still trailing me. I put the car in the garage and carried my stuff to the main house. When I got back to the garage, Granetti was there.

I spent the afternoon taking vending machines apart and putting them together again. Then I went back to the house and cleaned up, had a few drinks and a good dinner, and watched a movie.

The rest of the two weeks went pretty much the same. I'd get up and take a swim. After breakfast I'd go fishing. Then

I'd have a session with either Haywood or Mays, have lunch, and spend my afternoon with Granetti. He and I did have one more night out with Carol and Connie, but the rest of the evenings were spent drinking or watching a movie or television. By the end of that time I felt I could go into making vending machines for myself.

Granetti drove me back to Chicago and let me out at the apartment that was in the name of Peter Miloff. Our Russians were still with us. I went out for dinner, but returned straight to the apartment and went to bed early. Everything was as memorized as it would ever be, and I was tired.

The next day I went to Fenner's camera store and bought the camera and tape recorder. When I got back to the apartment there was a package for me. It contained several cartons of cigarettes and a pen. All I had to do now was cool my heels. While I was waiting, a messenger arrived with two checks from the Brotherhood Coin Vending Company. By picking up the phone and asking, I discovered I could cash the checks without leaving the building. The service was great.

It was about two o'clock when the phone rang. I picked it up and said hello.

"I am calling," a man's voice said, "to tell you that Mr. Kirilenko wants you to know that your plane will leave from New York tomorrow afternoon."

"I'll be there," I said, "at the same hotel I was before."

He hung up. I called the hotel in New York and reserved the same suite I'd had earlier. Then I called the airline and made a reservation. I thought about it a minute and then called Merry Sanders in New York. I got an answering service. I gave her my name and asked if she could call me back in an hour. After that I started to pack.

Then the phone got busy. The first call was from Eddie Mays. "We hear you're leaving tomorrow," he said.

"From New York," I said. "I'm leaving here very shortly. I'll stay at the hotel in New York tonight."

"Okay. Good luck." He hung up.

The phone rang again a few minutes later. This time it was Granetti. "How'd you like to go out on the town tonight?" he asked. "A farewell party."

"I'd like it," I told him, "but I'm packing right now to catch a plane. Then tomorrow I take off from New York on the long flight."

"Sorry," he said. "I had a nice little chick picked out for you. Well—good luck."

"Thanks," I said.

I hung up and went back to the packing. It was about a half hour later when the phone rang again. I picked it up.

"Peter," she said, "this is Merry Sanders. It was so nice of you to call."

"I'm going to be in New York in a few hours and then I have to leave tomorrow," I said. "Are you free to have dinner with me tonight?"

"I'll be free," she said. "I told you that. Will you call me when you get in, or do you want me to call you?"

"I'll call. I'll be at the same hotel, but I'll phone you as soon as I get checked in."

"Okay. And thanks for calling, Peter."

I hung up and finished the packing. Then I had the desk

call a taxi and went downstairs with my luggage. The trip to the airport and then from the New York airport to the hotel took more time than the flight itself. But I finally reached the hotel and checked in.

I knew that I was again followed all the way, but I paid no attention. When I was in the room I ordered a drink from room service and had a fast shower and a shave. Then I called Merry Sanders. The answering service came on, but as soon as I had said who was calling, Merry cut in.

"Welcome back," she said.

"Thanks, honey. Want to have dinner with me?"

"Sure. When?"

"Whenever it's convenient for you. In about two hours?"

"That's fine."

"Want me to pick you up?"

"I'll meet you at your hotel," she said. "Shall I call you when I get there?"

"Meet me in the bar," I said.

There was enough time for me to take a brief nap, which I did. When I awakened, I got dressed and went down to the bar. I'd been there about fifteen minutes when she came in. She looked good. I bought her a drink and after that we went out to a restaurant. I had already made a reservation, again picking a spot where I wouldn't be apt to run into anyone who knew Milo March. It was a nice evening—or night.

I didn't have much sleep, but I felt good when I awakened the next morning. I called room service and ordered a double martini, scrambled eggs and ham, and a pot of coffee. I finished all of that and was just beginning to feel that I might survive the morning when the phone rang. It was a voice with a Russian accent telling me what time a car would call for me.

I made it. I was down in the lobby with my luggage and all checked out by the time they told me that there was a car waiting for Mr. Miloff. With a bellhop leading the way, I paraded out front where a limousine was standing. There was a uniformed chauffeur behind the wheel and diplomatic plates on the car. My bags were stowed away; I tipped the bellhop and got into the rear door. I looked through the back window as we pulled away. For once, I wasn't being followed.

We reached Kennedy Airport and I went through all the formalities and finally ended up on board a huge Russian plane. I presumed my luggage was already stowed away on the ship. I was the only passenger on a plane built to carry over a hundred. There was full crew and a beautiful stewardess, who came back to ask if I wanted a drink before we even got off the ground. I wanted one. In fact, I needed one at that moment. I felt a little like a man who starts to cross the Atlantic alone in a rowboat.

The big jet took off and we were soon in the air and headed, I presumed, for Russia. The pretty stewardess came back again to assure me that she was there to cater to all of my needs—except possibly one—and to ask what did I want at the moment. I had another drink and lit a cigarette.

During the hours that followed, I had more to drink, quite a bit to eat, watched the stewardess wiggle up and down the aisle, and slept a couple of times. The time seemed to drag out endlessly, but we finally came down in Moscow.

There was quite a delegation to meet me. It turned out

that most of them were from the Automatic Machine Trust, although there were a few on the edge of the crowd who looked like they might be security policemen. There were several flowery speeches in Russian, which I answered in the same language, and then I was hustled out to a limousine and we drove off. I was in the back seat with one big, burly man, and there were two more like him in the front seat. By this time I had not the slightest idea who any of them were.

"What about my luggage?" I asked the man sitting with me.

"It will be delivered to you almost as soon as you arrive."

"Arrive where?"

He laughed. "We are providing you with an apartment on Proletarsky Rayone. I think you will find it very comfortable. It is one of the apartment houses where we lodge many of the people from the foreign embassies. It should be a congenial place for you."

"You are very kind," I said.

"There will be," he said, "an official party welcoming you to Moscow within a day or two, but it was thought that you might be tired after your trip and would prefer to rest until tomorrow. That is why we are driving you directly to your apartment."

I said something else polite, but I wasn't certain that he was telling the truth. I had been in Moscow before and I knew the section where he was taking me. It seemed to me that we were going a little out of the way, so that it couldn't be called exactly a direct route. I didn't, however, mention this.

In the meantime he continued to babble about how honored they were that I had agreed to come to help them, and he was sure that we would get along splendidly. For the most part I merely grunted in response. He had suggested that I was tired, so I played along with that for the time being.

Finally, after touring most of Moscow, we arrived at the apartment buildings on People's Street. My companion escorted me out of the car while the other two men stayed in the front street. We entered one of the buildings and went up to the second floor. He used a key to unlock a door and then presented the key to me with a flourish.

"This is your home while you are in the Soviet Union," he said, "and this is your key." He threw the door open, and the first thing I saw was my luggage sitting in the middle of the floor. "Ah," he said, "they have already delivered your luggage. We are very efficient in the Soviet Union."

"I am impressed," I said as he followed me into the apartment. I had tried to keep the irony out of my voice.

I looked around. All I could see at the moment was the living room, but it looked very nice. There was obviously more to the place than this, since I could see two doors opening off from it. That was better than I had expected.

"You will find everything here," he said. "There is even some food in the kitchen. Tomorrow, let us know what you want and it will be delivered. There are also some very nice restaurants not far from here, if you wish to eat out. We will also arrange for any other pleasures you wish while you're here." He sounded a little bit like a pimp.

"Thanks."

"Now I will leave you to rest," he said. He handed me a slip of paper with some writing on it. "This is the address of the office where you will come tomorrow. Do you wish to have us pick you up with a car?"

"I think not," I said. "I should be able to find it by asking questions. Then perhaps we can make some definite arrangements later. I would prefer, if possible, to get a driving license and have access to a small car."

"I'm sure it can be arranged," he said with a smile. "Then we will see you tomorrow. If you wish anything, there is a phone number on the paper I gave you. You may call at any time. There is a telephone in your apartment. I trust you will rest well."

"Thank you."

I watched as he left the apartment and closed the door. I went to look around. There was a good-sized kitchen and a large bedroom in addition to the living room. When I had finished going over all of it, I went back to the kitchen. The refrigerator contained such things as caviar and smoked salmon and fruit juices. There was also a loaf of black bread, and in the cupboard there were several bottles of vodka. So I mixed a drink. Then I walked around the apartment with the glass in one hand and my special fountain pen in the other. According to its indicator, there were three microphones in the apartment.

There was one in the cupboard of the kitchen, one in a table lamp in the living room, and one in the bedroom ceiling light directly over the bed. I couldn't find anything else.

I carried my luggage into the bedroom, put down my drink, and unpacked. My cigarettes, the camera, and the tape recorder were there and seemed to be exactly as they were when packed. I put everything away and then finished my drink. After that I took a nap.

When I awakened, I took a shower and changed clothes. Then I turned out the lights and left the apartment. I was certain that I was being followed, but I didn't bother trying to check on it. I walked until I came to a restaurant that looked like it might be all right, went in, and picked out a table. A waiter came over and I ordered a vodka.

I was about halfway through it when my attention was attracted to a girl who was at another table. She stood up, starting to leave. She was a pretty girl with long blond hair and a beautiful figure. She appeared to be slightly drunk. As she reached my table she stopped and looked me over.

"You must be an American," she said in Russian.

I smiled at her. "I was hoping it wouldn't show. May I buy you a vodka?"

"No, but you may buy me a double vodka, since all Americans are rich."

Well, that was fast. It was a recognition signal and meant that she was one of the double agents I was to meet in Moscow. I would have been happier if she had waited a few days.

SIX

I looked at her again. She was certainly no more than twenty-five. She was wearing a trench coat, but it failed to conceal her curves. There was an accent to her Russian, so she was probably from another Communist country. The chief question was whether or not she was a trap. There was only one way to find out.

"Sit down," I said with what I hoped was a proper leer if anyone was watching. I beckoned to the waiter and ordered two double vodkas.

"I was about to have something to eat?" I said. "Would you join me?"

"I would enjoy that," she said.

The waiter brought the drinks and went away. "I am Peter Miloff," I said.

"Marya Rijekta," she responded. She lifted her glass to me. "It is not too safe to talk here," she added softly. "Later, we can take a walk and talk to each other."

"All right. To your health, Marya."

We had two more drinks and then some very good food. We finished with tea and pastries. I paid the bill and we walked out and started down the street.

"We are being followed," she said.

"I imagine that you are usually followed."

She giggled. "You are gallant. There is park near here. I suggest that we go there and sit on a bench while we're getting acquainted. That way, no one can get too near us."

"That sounds nice. Let's go."

We walked to the park and entered it. The lighting was good, and I noticed a man enter shortly after we did and sit on a bench some distance from us. He pretended to be enjoying the evening, but I decided he was probably our shadow.

"Who are you, Peter?" she asked.

I felt like a Boy Scout who had just been asked what kind of knots he could tie. "Uncle Vanya," I said.

"I'm Orloff's Wife," she said.

So she was either for real or the Russians had our whole scam broken down. I had no choice but to go along with it.

"How come you contacted me so quickly?" I asked.

She hesitated. "Do you know what I do?" she asked.

"You work for the Yugoslavian embassy and are also an agent for your government."

She sighed. "It's a little more complicated than that. I am also an agent for the Soviet Union. I was ordered to accept if I was approached by the Russians. As you know, I also work for the CIA."

"That's really moonlighting," I said. I looked at her and wondered who she really worked for. "I won't ask the obvious question. You haven't answered my first question yet. Why did you contact me so soon?"

"I was ordered to get acquainted with you by the Russians. I followed you from your apartment to the restaurant. So did the man who is sitting on the bench over there."

"I knew about him, but I confess I didn't know about you. How did they happen to pick you for the job?"

"I'm often used to check on visiting foreigners," she said. She sounded sad. "I guess it's because they think there will not be so much suspicion of me, since I am not Russian. And then I am a woman."

"And a very lovely one."

"Thank you, Peter." She touched my hand for a minute.

"How did you happen to start working for us?"

"James Hartwell." Something about her voice made me look at her.

"In love with him?"

She laughed. "Oh, no. Everything he said made such good sense and he was very nice. I was fond of him."

"You worked with him?"

"Yes."

"Doing what?"

"Trying to find a man named Richard Sorge. But I was never able to learn anything about him."

"What happened to Hartwell?" I asked.

She shook her head. "He just disappeared. I've never heard anything about him since then. But I don't have many places to get information like that."

"One of the things I have to do is find Hartwell," I said. "I also want to find out about Richard Sorge."

"I'll try again," she said. Then she sighed. "We'd better not sit here too long. And I'd like a drink."

"Where would you like to go?"

"We'd better go to your apartment. That is what they will

expect. Don't forget they assigned me to pick you up. But I must tell you that there will probably be listening devices somewhere in the apartment."

"There are three of them, one in each room. I have already located them. But I can tell you about vending machines and you can tell me about your home country. If you think it'll make the Russians happy, I can make a pass at you and you can reject me and go home indignantly."

She laughed. "I'm not sure the Russians would like that. And I don't have far to go. I live in the same building. I share an apartment with another girl who works at the embassy."

"All right. Let's go."

I took her hand as we walked out of the park. It would probably please the man who was following. We walked back to our building and went into my apartment.

"Oh," she said as we entered, "they gave you a very nice place. It's lovely."

"It's comfortable," I said. I wasn't going to give them any free praise.

"You must be a rich American capitalist!"

I laughed at her. "I'm not rich, baby, and there are no poor capitalists. What do you want to drink?"

"Vodka. What else?"

"Come into the kitchen. I think there are a few other things." I led the way to the kitchen and opened the cupboard. In addition to the vodka, there was brandy, some wine, and several bottles of imported whiskey.

"You must be rich," she said, "to have so much to drink. But

I'll have the vodka. You go sit down and I will fix the drinks. What do you want?"

"Vodka and fruit juice," I said.

I went back into the living room. There was a television set and a radio. I turned on the radio and found a station with music, then sat down and lit a cigarette.

She came in with the two drinks and sat down next to me. We drank and talked. I told her a little about vending machines for the benefit of the microphone and then asked her about Yugoslavia. We had several more drinks. I leaned over and kissed her. She returned it with more enthusiasm I had expected.

I had already decided that the Russians must have wanted this meeting to end in only one way. The question had to do with their picture of me. They were certain I was a member of a slightly shady group in American society, and they would expect me to react in a specific way. I had already decided to give them what they wanted. But Marya's kiss convinced me that it might be as much pleasure as duty.

We had another drink, then I took her by the hand and led her into the bedroom. We both knew about the microphone, but after a while we forgot about it. Anything we said didn't have political meaning anyway. I remembered thinking, just before I went to sleep, that the KGB man assigned to monitor the microphones must be a man who liked to peek through keyholes.

She was still asleep when I awakened. There was a child-like expression on her face. I checked the time and decided I could let her sleep a few more minutes. I went into the bathroom and had a shower. When I came out, I made a more thorough check of the kitchen. There were a lot of tasty things, but nothing that I fancied for breakfast. I settled that problem by having a vodka and fruit juice with my morning cigarette. Then I went back to the bedroom. Marya was still asleep.

I sat on the edge of the bed and stroked her arm until she began to show signs of waking up. Then I put my other hand gently over her mouth. When her eyes opened they were filled with fear, and the first place she looked was at the lamp where the microphone was concealed. They shifted and she looked at me and the fear began to fade. I took my hand away from her mouth.

"Good morning, Marya," I said.

"Good morning, Peter," she answered. She stretched and smiled. "It's a wonderful morning," she added.

"That's what I was thinking too. But there's one thing wrong with it."

She looked at me uncertainly. "What?"

"There's nothing in the kitchen that looks good for breakfast. If you'll hurry, there'll be time to take you out before we both have to go to work."

She leaped out of bed. Her body was even more lovely than I remembered from the night before. She slipped on her dress and her shoes and gathered up the rest of her clothes and her bag. "I'll be right back," she said. She hurried out of the apartment before I could answer.

I went back to the bathroom and shaved. I got dressed and made myself another vodka and juice and sat down to wait for her. I was halfway through it when there was a soft knock on the door. I opened it and there she was. She had certainly done a good job in such a short time, for she looked radiant.

"Was I too long, Peter?" she asked.

"No. I hadn't even finished my vodka. Let me drink it and we'll eat."

She came into the apartment. "The man who drinks in the morning is not to be trusted," she said with a smile.

"On the contrary, Marya, it is the man who drinks at night who is not to be trusted. By the way, you look very pretty— but I think you were even prettier when you first leaped out of bed."

"You will spoil me with such flattery. Come on, or I will be late for work."

I finished the vodka and we left. When we reached the street I noticed that we immediately had company behind us. But he was too far away to hear our casual conversation.

"Marya," I said, "I neglected to ask you something last night. You said that the Russians assigned you to pick me up. But when you first approached me in the restaurant you used the recognition code. How did you know that I was the right one?"

"I received a message that a new agent was coming, that his name was Peter Miloff, code name Uncle Vanya, and that I was to be subject to his orders."

"Who told you this?"

"I don't know. There is a drop in Kremlin Park where I get messages. It was there, fastened beneath a bench. When I was ordered to pick you up, I was told your name and that you were an American. I thought you had to be the one, so I tried the code sentence on you."

We went into a small restaurant not far from the apartment building. While we ordered, I was thinking. They hadn't told me that any of the double agents would get in touch with me. I had assumed that when I was ready I would get in touch with them. Now I wondered if the other three agents would also be contacting me. I wasn't too happy about it.

After breakfast, which was fine except for the tea instead of coffee, we both had to leave without too much lingering.

"Marya," I said, "I don't know what's going to happen today. I don't even know if I'll still be in Moscow by tonight. If I'm free, I'd like to see you again tonight, but I can't make any plans. I have to do a lot of work for the Automatic Machine Trust and try to sandwich in the other work I must do."

"I understand," she said. "I also am never sure where I will be, but I think I will be home tonight. If you are free, just come and knock on my door. If I am not there, my roommate will tell you that I won't be home until very late or tell you exactly what time I will be back."

I patted her arm and went to look for a taxi. I found one so quickly that I suspected the driver was also a plant. This feeling was strengthened when I noticed my faithful shadow had dropped out of the picture.

I was delivered to a large, modern building. The sign on the front said that it was the Automatic Machine Trust Building. I paid the driver, went inside, and found the office that was noted on the slip of paper I had been given the night before. The man who had escorted me to my apartment was there, sitting behind a desk.

"Ah, Miloff," he said. "You are very prompt. In the confusion of your arrival you have probably forgotten my name. It is Nikolai Ivanov. Please sit down. I will take you to your own office soon."

I took the chair next to his desk and lit a cigarette.

"You like your apartment?" he asked.

"It is fine."

"I am glad to see," he continued, "that you have already experienced some of our social life. That is good."

"What do you mean?" I asked.

He smiled at me. "You met a young lady from one of the embassies in Moscow. You walked in the park, then returned to the building in which you are living. She also had breakfast with you this morning. I am glad that you are finding a social life here so quickly."

"What's the idea?" I asked. I tried to hit just the right tone of indignation. "Do you mean that I'm being followed?"

He waved his hand in a friendly way. "Of course not, my dear friend. I think I told you that your building is occupied by many diplomatic persons and others who are important—such as yourself. As a result, we do keep guards on the building all the time for the protection of those who live there. Since you were new, there was a report made. But you may be assured that they will not interfere with your private life while you are here."

"I hope not," I said, and left it at that. "When do we go to work?"

"Officially you are already at work. But since we are starting from the ground up, it may take a few days to get started. Do you have anything that you wish to do before devoting your full time to work?"

"No. I think I'm supposed to get in touch with the American Embassy and let them know I'm here and where I'm staying, but I imagine I can do that at any time."

"Why don't you do that sometime today?" he suggested. "In the meantime there is a Soviet driving license waiting for you in your office. And there is a Pobeda downstairs which will be yours to use while you are with us."

"Thank you."

"You will work primarily with me," he said, "although at times you may feel it necessary to work with some of our engineers and production people. Now, we would like to ask a favor of you."

"What?"

"The editors of *Pravda* would like to run a series of articles on the plans for these automatic machines. There is a list of possible locations in Moscow, and there is a journalist now waiting in your office who would like to accompany you during a preliminary tour of these spots. It is possible that the journalist might also wish to accompany you on visits to other Soviet cities."

"That's all right with me," I said. "But let me ask you something now. All I know is that you want to install what we call coin vending machines. We have many kinds. Some are used for gambling; some for the playing of games; some for dispensing food, hot and cold drinks, candy, cigarettes, newspapers and magazines, and even for playing records. And that's only the beginning. What do you want?"

"We do not have any limitations at the moment. I believe that priority might be given to those machines that will dispense food, drinks, and newspapers; but we might wish to go further. We will be guided by your recommendations. I imagine that to some degree it would depend on the location of the machines."

"Yes," I said. "But you'll have to tell me what you want and then I will tell you how to do it. Let's go meet your journalist."

"Follow me," he said.

He got up and walked around the desk. I followed him out of the office and down the corridor to another office. He opened the door and marched inside, with me behind him. It was not quite as nice as his office, but it was still pretty good. There was a third person there, a girl. She was small but well shaped and had long black hair.

"Irina Simonova," the man said, "may I present Peter Miloff, the American who has come to help us with the automatic machines."

"Hello," I said blankly. "Do you mean that you're the … ?"

"Comrade Simonova," the man said, "is a journalist for *Pravda*."

My head was beginning to spin. Unless there was a coincidence, this was another one of the agents I was supposed to contact when I needed her. The service was too good.

"I am honored," I said—mostly because I couldn't think of anything else to say.

"I will leave you two together to plan a series of articles," Nikolai Ivanov said. "You will find your driving license and a Soviet identity card in the center drawer of your desk, Mr. Miloff. When you are finished, you will come back to see me." He beamed at both of us and left.

I went around and sat behind the desk. I opened the drawer, and sure enough there were the two cards. I put them in my pocket and looked at the girl. She was smiling at me.

"I hope you don't mind," she said. "Our readers will be very interested in the project on which you are helping us."

"I don't mind," I said. "But I haven't really started yet and I don't have any idea about what is wanted or needed, or where the machines will be installed."

"I have a list of the suggested places. We can visit them and you can give me your opinions as to what might be built for each place. Are you free today?"

"Yes. I do have to report to the American Embassy, but I can't think of anything else, except that I want to do some shopping during the day."

She glanced at her watch. "Why don't you take care of those things and then meet me at the offices of *Pravda?* Do you know where we are?"

"No, but I'm sure that I can find it."

"You shouldn't have any trouble. You speak our language very well. I will see you later." She smiled again and left.

I sat at my desk and looked around. It was a pleasant-looking office, carpeted, and with a couple of scenic photographs on the walls. There was a file cabinet, two chairs in addition to the one behind the desk, and of course a phone. The desk drawers held all kinds of paper and pencils and pens. Pretending to make some notes, I used the pen I'd brought with me to test for bugs. That didn't take long. There was a listening device in the telephone.

I went downstairs and found the Pobeda. As I was starting

the motor, I again used the pen. I got no evidence that the car was bugged. I'd go over it more thoroughly, however, before I did any extensive talking in it.

A traffic policeman gave me directions, and I drove to the American Embassy. After a short wait I was shown into the office of some minor official. He looked at my passport.

"Oh, yes, Mr. Miloff," he said. "We were informed that you were coming here to do some work. I don't recall exactly what."

"Consultant to the Automatic Machine Trust. They want to learn how to make coin vending machines."

"That's interesting," he said blankly. "Well, the State Department has given its approval. How are they treating you?"

"Fine. I have a very nice apartment in Proletarsky Rayone and an office in the Trust Building."

"Good. If there's anything we can do to help you, just let us know. By the way, there is one thing."

"What?"

"We now have somewhat better relations with the Soviet government, and we are advising American nationals to be careful not to do anything that might damage this. In a way, every American here is an unofficial ambassador."

"I'll try to remember that, sir," I said. I knew he didn't have the slightest idea why I was really there, and I didn't want to disillusion him.

He stood up and shook my hand. "If you run into any problems, just get in touch with us."

I went back to the Pobeda and drove to the neighborhood of

my apartment building. I soon found some stores and bought additional things I wanted for the kitchen. I took them to the apartment. I went back to the car and drove off, but this time I made certain that I was not being followed. When I was sure, I headed for a section of Moscow that I remembered from the time when I had been there before.

There was a little restaurant just a couple of blocks off Gorky Street. I found it without too much trouble. I wanted to buy some rubles on the black market, even though I had plenty of rubles at the moment and wouldn't have any trouble getting more. But I wanted to have some money they didn't know about. It was several years since I had been in Moscow, but I had an idea that the same operator I'd known then would still be around. If not, there'd probably be another one.

I parked the car and walked to the restaurant. There was no one in front of it. When I entered, there were a few people there, but I didn't see the man I was looking for. I took a table and ordered a vodka.

"I have been away from the city," I said to the waiter. "Is Nuritdin still around?"

"Not today," the waiter said. He didn't remain for any more conversation.

I sipped my vodka and looked around the room. Then I noticed that there was a man staring at me. He was a big, burly man with a face that looked as if somebody had been working on it. But there was something about the way he dressed that looked more American than Russian.

Then, suddenly, he was on his feet and walking directly toward me. All I could do was fervently hope that I wasn't going to meet another double agent. He stopped when he reached my table.

"Hi, pal," he said in English. "You're from the States, right?"

"Right," I said.

"From Chicago?"

"Yes."

He grinned and pulled out a chair and sat down without waiting for an invitation. He waved his hand in the air and the waiter came over with a drink for him and another vodka for me.

"I don't think I heard your name," I said.

He laughed loudly. "I didn't tell you yet. I'm Georgi Zoubov."

"So?"

"You're Pete Miloff and you work for Angelo Benotti in Chi. Right?"

"Where'd you pick all this up?" I asked.

"I used to live in Chicago. I worked for Benotti. I was like part of his family. You understand?"

"Yeah."

"I came over here for a visit a couple of years ago," he went on, "and these damned squares won't let me go back. But I still get word from Chi and I heard that you was coming over to teach these peasants how to make a slot machine. Some laugh, huh?"

"Yeah," I said. "What do you do for action over here?"

"I got a few things going for me," he said, winking. "Now that you're here, I can do a few things for you and you can do a few things for me. A couple of smart racket boys ought to be able to take over this whole town."

SEVEN

This whole thing was beginning to feel like a secret meeting held in the middle of Red Square. It was bad enough that I had been in Moscow less than twenty-four hours and two of the double agents I was supposed to contact had already found their way to me, but now it was a Syndicate man who thought I was one of his buddies. I had a few choice thoughts about General Sam Roberts; I kept them to myself.

"You're probably right," I said, "but I won't have much time to take over anything. And I'm being watched pretty closely. I managed to lose the tail today to come here, but I don't know how often I can do it. Now I want to ask a couple of questions."

"Shoot."

"You say you knew my name and that I was coming over. How did you find out?"

"I got a connection I give a few rubles to and he slips me information about Americans who are coming in. He told me that the Automatic Machine gang here was bringing in a guy from Chicago who was with the Mob. He got your name for me and when you'd get here. Another connection of mine works at the airport. He told me last night that you'd come in, and he gave me a sort of description of you. When you came in here, you looked like the guy he described. And them threads you're wearing had to come from the States. We don't get many Americans in this joint. Then you asked for Nuritdin and that clinched it."

"How?"

"Nobody asks for Nuritdin if they're looking for something legit. So I figured it had to be you. As soon as you told me you was an American and from Chi, I knew I was right. What do you want with Nuritdin?"

"How do I know you're what you say you are?" I asked.

He nodded as though to admit that was a proper question. "Ask me any question you want to about Chicago."

"You say you know Benotti. You ever been to his house?"

"Yeah. I was there a couple of times when he was planning a hit."

"Okay. Describe Benotti to me and the room where you met."

He gave me a pretty accurate description of Benotti and then a good one of his study.

"Did you know," I asked when he'd finished, "Benotti's driver?"

"The one when I was there was Granetti. Bob, but the old man called him Roberto. A tough boy, especially with a gun. And a great one for the broads."

I didn't underestimate the KGB, but I doubted if they could have an agent with that sort of information. So Zoubov was for real. It didn't make me feel any easier. In fact, it was probably a new threat for me. I could only hope that he didn't have connections with which to get messages to and from Chicago.

"Okay," I said. "I guess you've been there. But I have to be careful. These guys are worse than the cops back home."

"You ain't kidding," he said. "How come you know Nuritdin?"

"I have some connections, too," I said with a smile. "You know Nuritdin well?"

"Sure. Ever since I been stuck in this damn place. Why did you want to see him?"

"I want to sell some American dollars," I said bluntly.

"He ought to be back in an hour or so."

"I don't think I can wait that long. I'll have to try to catch him again."

"I do a lot of business with Nuritdin," he said, "so I don't want to cut him out of anything, but if you don't get in touch with him, I might get the sale for you."

"I'll try to get back tonight. I can't be sure that I can make it. And I want something else."

"What?"

"A piece."

He whistled softly. "That's not impossible, but it ain't easy. What kind do you want?"

"I don't like them," I said, "but I guess it'll have to be an automatic. Something not too big—but big enough to stop a man—and fairly flat."

"I might get you one, possibly a Hungarian make. Roughly, a thirty-eight. It'll be expensive."

"Okay."

He nodded. "I should be able to have it by tomorrow. Where can I reach you?"

I smiled. "You can't. They put me in an apartment house that's watched all the time and is bugged. They've given me an office that's bugged. I'll have to get in touch with you when I can. Are you usually here?"

"Every day at some time or other. The gun will probably run a hundred and fifty bucks."

I finished my second vodka and put down money for the waiter. "That's fine," I said. "I'll see you as soon as I can." I got up and walked out.

A traffic officer gave me directions, so it didn't take me long to reach the building that housed *Pravda*. I parked and went in and asked for Irina Simonova. I was told to wait. She showed up in a couple of minutes.

"That was fast," she said. "We can take a taxi if you like. *Pravda* will pay for it."

"I have a car—provided by the government."

"Good," she said.

We left the building and started for the place I had parked the car.

"Uncle Vanya," she said softly, as we walked along the sidewalk, "I'm Masha."

"I know," I said.

"I wanted to make the contact here because there aren't many places where we can talk, not even in your car."

"I've partly checked it and it seems to be clean, but we'd better not."

"We'll find a place later," she said, just before we reached the car.

We visited all sorts of places, ranging from the big state department store to small stores, restaurants, sporting centers, and even sidewalk newsstands. I dutifully made notes at each spot and told her what sort of machines might be installed there. We were so busy that before I was aware of the time it was beginning to get dark.

"Well," she said, putting her own notes away, "I think we've done enough for today. If you're free, why don't we have dinner together? I think *Pravda* will be willing to pay for it."

"We'll have dinner together on one condition," I said. "I'll pay for it. Your government is paying me very well."

"All right. Where would you like to go?"

"It's your town. Someplace where the food is good. And don't worry about the cost."

"Then we'll go to Praga."

I had been there before, but I let her tell me how to reach it and didn't let on that I knew the place. It was an excellent restaurant and had better service than most of those in Russia. We were shown to a table in the rear of the room with our backs to the wall. We ordered two vodkas.

"Peter," she said in a low voice when the waiter had delivered the drinks and left. "This should be a safe place to talk, but I think we'd better wait. When you take me home we can talk in my apartment."

"Is that any safer?" I asked.

"I'm certain there are no listening devices there." She smiled at me. "Because of my job, I am very much trusted."

"And this is not safe?"

"Normally, yes," she said. "But there is another reason tonight to suspect it. Don't look immediately, but glance in a few minutes at the man who is at a table directly across from us. He is alone."

I lifted my glass to touch hers and drank. As I put the glass down, I looked at the man. He was fairly young, heavyset, with a rather nice face.

"Who is he?" I asked.

"He is the KGB, but it may be only an accident that he is here. His name is Grigory Masinov."

I didn't believe in accidents, especially ones like this, for Masinov was another of the double agents I was supposed to contact if I needed him. I was beginning to feel that I had an embarrassment of little helpers. But I didn't mention this to her.

We had a few more drinks and then a very good dinner, starting with caviar. What else when you're in Russia? After dinner, we had coffee. It wasn't the greatest, but it was better than tea, and the brandy helped. Finally I paid the bill and we left. I was relieved to notice that Masinov wasn't showing any signs of leaving.

We had driven several blocks before she said anything. I'd been aware that she was looking back fairly frequently. I had also checked, and was pretty certain that we weren't being followed.

"It's such a nice night," she said finally. "I'd like to stop for a few minutes. Do you know the lovely parks we have in Moscow?"

"No," I said truthfully.

When I'd been in Moscow before, I'd been too busy to indulge in park watching, so my only experience had been last night. I wondered if she was thinking of a park as a way to spot a tail.

She gave me directions and finally told me to pull in near what was obviously a park. "This," she said, "is Kremlin Park. It is beautiful. I often come here at night by myself."

We got out and went in. It was almost empty. There were two couples on benches at some distance from each other and that was all. We walked along and I was remembering that this was the park where we had a drop for our agents. I wondered if that had anything to do with her wanting to visit it.

We were finally in the center of the park when she put her hand on my arm. "Do you mind if we sit here for just a moment?" she asked. "I know it's silly, but it always makes me feel restful to stay here for a few minutes when the day is over."

"I don't mind," I said.

We sat down on the bench. It was a beautiful park and we were sitting where we could immediately spot anyone who followed us. But I didn't have any confidence that a Soviet agent would be foolish enough to show himself. I took out two cigarettes and lit them, then passed one to her.

She took it, but she was squirming around on the bench as if it were uncomfortable. I had an idea. This particular bench was probably the place where a drop was made and she must have been trying to discover if there was a message for her.

I smoked my cigarette and pretended to be fascinated by the view. But I knew I was right when I saw her holding her hand down beside her leg and glancing at it. Then she lifted her head and looked around the park. There was no one near us.

"Peter," she said.

I pretended to be startled out of my courtship with nature and looked at her. "Yes, Irina?"

"This is for you," she said, handing me a small square of paper. It was very thin and had been folded many times, and it was sealed. On one side "Uncle Vanya" was written in Russian. I tore the seal, unfolded the paper, and held it in my cupped hand so that only I could see it. There were two sentences and a name:

We have information that one of the four double agents is not to be trusted. We do not yet know which one. Uncle Bobby.

The code meant that it came from Washington. I crumpled the paper up and used my cigarette to burn it. I ground the ashes under my foot.

"We'd better go," Irina said. She sounded nervous.

I nodded and we went back to the car. I would have liked to stop by the restaurant in hope of catching Zoubov or Nuritdin, but decided it wasn't a good idea. I was pretty sure that there weren't any bugs in the car I'd been given, but there could have been a beeper that could be picked up by another car several blocks away and would let them know when, and approximately where, we had stopped. I followed Irina's directions to get to her apartment.

We ended up in another section of Moscow I had known before. It was Kotelnicheskaye Embankment. At Irina's direction, I parked in front of a large, modern apartment building. The ground floor was mostly stores, and it didn't look much different from many such buildings in New York City.

"Irina," I said, as we got out of the car, "do you have anything to drink in your apartment?"

"Vodka."

"When we enter, ask me if I'd like a drink and I will say that I would. Then make as much noise as you can fixing the drinks until I give you a signal."

"All right," she said.

We went into the building and up to the fourth floor. She used her key to open the door and we stepped inside. It was small but comfortable and large enough to show that she had an important job.

"This is where I live, Peter," she said. "Would you like a drink?"

"Vodka," I said. "You can give me a glass of water with it, too, if you don't mind."

"Make yourself comfortable. It will be ready in a minute."

She went into the kitchen and turned on the water. There were other noises almost immediately. I pulled out my pen and went to work. I covered the entire apartment very quickly, but the pen never lit up, so I decided that she was right in thinking her place wasn't bugged. I went into the kitchen and nodded.

She stopped making all the noise and handed me a drink. I lifted it. *"Zah vahsheh zdolirohvyeh,"* I said.

"To your health," she repeated. "All right?"

"Seems to be," I said. "I went over everything and there didn't seem to be any listening devices."

"I was certain there weren't any," she said. "Let's go into the other room."

I followed her. "Now," I said, "tell me one thing. Why did you get in touch with me?"

She looked surprised. "I was told to. I had a message at the drop telling me that an agent named Peter Miloff was arriving to work as a consultant to the Automatic Machine Trust and that I was to work with him. I arranged to do a series of stories on your work so it would be easier for us to be together."

"Who told you about me?"

"I don't know. It was signed with the code name of Sasha. I get all my messages from him."

"He's got a big mouth," I said sourly. "Are you really going to print these stories about the work I'm going to do here?"

"Of course. With pictures."

"No!" I said sharply. "Even if you have to blow up the plant, you must not print any pictures of me."

"All right," she said. "I think I can arrange that."

"You'd better, honey."

"Why?"

"Because if you print my picture, the whole thing is going to blow up in our faces. Who did you work with before I came here?"

"Sasha and Nikita. Those were their code names. Once I had a message at the drop from Orloff's Wife. Most of my messages have been from Sasha."

"Did you ever meet any of them?"

"Only Nikita once. I've never met the others. When I could, I supplied what they wanted through the same drop." She suddenly looked frightened. "Oh! I forgot something!"

"What?"

"That message for you—when one is picked up. A red chalk mark is supposed to be made beneath a bench in Gorky Park when the message has been picked up."

"I know about that. I'll do it on my way home. Do you still get messages from Nikita?"

"No. The last one was a least three months ago."

"Who was Nikita?"

She hesitated for a moment. "I only met him once, but he told me his name was James Hartwell."

I sighed. There were times when I wondered how agents could be so stupid. But in this case I was glad that he had been, since I at least knew that she, too, had worked with him.

"What were you working on for him?"

"To try to find a man named Richard Sorge."

"Did you have any success?"

She shook her head. "He was a Soviet agent during World War II, but he was arrested and executed. I can't very well go around asking questions about him now. I got that much out of the files. That's all there is on him. He was not a native Russian, you know."

"I know," I said. "What happened to James Hartwell?" I asked bluntly.

"I don't know," she said. "He must have been arrested, but we haven't had any information about him since. I imagine he's probably in prison somewhere and it's being kept quiet."

"It certainly is. Do you think you could find some way to check on him?"

"I'll try," she said uncertainly, "but I can't be sure how much success I'll have. I can get any information I need when it is related to a story I'm doing. If it's not, all I will accomplish is to draw attention to myself without learning anything. They don't like us to go around asking questions about things that do not concern us. Sometimes I overhear things, but I haven't been able to on any of these things."

"Well," I said, taking a deep breath, "first I want to tell you that I am not a regular agent, although I am an agent on this one assignment. Normally, I work for an outfit in America that makes vending machines. Although such machines are legal there, they are controlled by what is known as organized crime."

"Does that mean that you are a gangster?" she asked.

"Some people think I am," I said truthfully. "But that doesn't necessarily make it true."

"I know. I was just surprised. My orders are to work with you, so nothing else is important."

She stood up and took my glass, went into the kitchen, and came back with two fresh drinks.

"I have two assignments," I told her. "One is to find out where James Hartwell is—if he's still alive. The other is to learn if Richard Sorge is alive and active—and if the Fourth Bureau is still active, under that name or another."

She frowned. "As I said, I haven't been able to find out anything about James Hartwell. If he's still alive, he could be in any one of a hundred prisons."

"There's no way you can check on it?"

"I don't think so. I thought about this before. The paper wouldn't think of running a series on political prisoners, which is about the only way I could ask questions leading to a single prisoner. There has never been anything about Hartwell in any of the papers, so there is no place I can start without revealing I have information which I shouldn't have."

"I know," I said. "We don't want you to run too big a risk of exposing yourself. What about the Fourth Bureau?"

She thought for a moment. "When I looked up Richard Sorge, it was mentioned. I think it was a Red Army Intelligence operation."

"It was. Later it became a joint operation between the Red Army and the state secret police. We haven't heard anything about it since Sorge supposedly died. But there is a feeling that it's still operating and with Sorge at the head of it."

"Wouldn't he be terribly old now?"

"Not as old as you might think. About the same age as Khrushchev."

"There isn't anything in our files on Sorge beyond his death. Maybe I could suggest a series on Soviet heroes who are not well known, and if they approve of it, that would permit me to look into other files about Sorge."

"All right. Try it. In the meantime, I might be able to get another lead."

"Maybe another agent," she said. "You must have other agents here ..."

"Probably," I said.

She went to replenish our drinks again. "We'll be working together for several days," she said, as she came back, "so we'll be able to compare notes at some time or other."

"Sure. It will be nice working with you anyway. But remember—no pictures of me."

"I'll remember. There won't be any problem about that. They'd rather not glorify an American."

"And this American would rather not be glorified. Well, we'll take it the way it comes. How did you happen to start working for us?"

She hesitated. "I think it was my father, but I only realized that recently. He was one of the people who was caught in a purge. He died in prison. Later, it was admitted that a mistake had been made about him, and the family was no longer under a cloud. When I finished school I was given a job at *Pravda*. I think I already had admiration for America, but one of my first assignments was to do a story about Americans in Moscow. I became very friendly with a girl who worked in your embassy, and she told me many stories about your country. I didn't use those in the story I wrote. Then a couple of years ago, I met an American journalist. One night, when I had dinner with him, he brought up the question of me being an American agent. I just laughed at the time, but I thought about it and changed my mind two weeks later."

"Why?" I asked.

"I'm not sure I can explain it, Peter. I was raised to believe that this is the best government in the world. What happened with my father upset me, but there have also been a lot of little things that disturbed me. I have liked things I heard about America. Your country is paying me for the work that I do. All the money is being put in a bank in America. ... Peter, do you think I will ever be able to go to your country?"

"Sure, honey," I said. "We'll work it out for you before this is over." I reached out and put my arm around her shoulders.

Suddenly she leaned over and her mouth was searching for mine. There was a frantic passion in her lips. My first thought was to wonder if Hartwell had at least experienced this before he went to prison—or death. Then I was caught up in the fire of her body and didn't think anymore.

Later, she fell asleep. I dressed and started to leave. I looked down at her. She was beautiful but, asleep, she looked very young and defenseless. I found something to cover her with, kissed her on the forehead, and left.

I would have liked to stop by the restaurant, but decided it was too late. I drove to within about four blocks of my apartment, then walked into Gorky Park. I had no trouble finding the right bench. I had a small piece of red chalk in my pocket for the purpose of acknowledging the pickup, so I used it to mark the bottom of the bench.

I went back to the car and drove to the building where I was living, parked, and got out.

"Comrade Miloff," a voice said from the darkness. "I trust that you had a pleasant evening and that you just enjoyed your short rest in the park."

EIGHT

Moving carefully, I locked the car. Then I straightened up and turned around. I could see the shadowy figure of someone standing beneath a tree.

"I prefer to see the person I'm speaking to," I said. "If you don't care to show yourself, I will go to my apartment. It is late and I have much work to do tomorrow."

He chuckled and stepped out where the streetlight showed his face. I sighed, partly from relief and partly from anger. It was the man Irina had pointed out to me in the restaurant.

"I am Grigory Masinov," he said, "of the KGB."

"That's very interesting," I said, "but I fail to see what it has to do with me."

"I am also sometimes known as Tolstoy. And you are Uncle Vanya."

"Thanks," I said dryly. "Tell me some more. Like why you come up to me with this story and why you're here now."

"It's nothing," he said. "I got a message from Sasha that you were going to be here on an important mission. I am to work under your orders. I have already arranged to be assigned to guard you and watch you. That will make it easier for us to talk. I waited for you tonight so that you will not be taken by surprise when I show up in your office tomorrow morning."

"That's all?" I asked.

"That's all for tonight."

"Then I'll see you tomorrow," I said shortly.

I turned and walked to the entrance of my building. I noticed that there was a guard on duty. He looked at me briefly and wrote something in a book in front of him. He was sitting in a small cubicle, which gave him a clear view of everyone entering or leaving the wing. I went on upstairs.

It was late, but the first thing I did was to make myself a good stiff drink. I turned on the radio and sat down to think. It was a hell of a situation. I was accustomed to working alone. Now I had been in Moscow only slightly more than one day and I was surrounded by agents—and a refugee gangster. Not only that, so far none of the agents knew a damned thing, but they were falling all over themselves getting to me instead of waiting for me to contact them. Then there was the message I'd gotten at the drop, which said that one of the four agents I was supposed to contact was not to be trusted.

Which one? If only one of the four had been eager to reach me, it might have been a lead. So far, three had already gotten to me, and I had a hunch the other one would appear soon. And one of them would be trying to set a trap. For me. I'd have to play that one out and try to spot which it was.

There was another problem that bothered me even more. Two of the agents, Marya and Irina, had no information at all on the things I needed to know. Even on the surface, it seemed unlikely that they would be able to provide any information. I hadn't really expected anything. I'd have to dig it up myself.

I already had an idea about Hartwell. It might work. But Sorge and the Fourth Bureau were another matter. I had no ideas about that at all. I thought of a few rude names for General Sam Roberts, finished my drink, and went to bed.

Despite only a few hours' sleep, I was up early. I felt my way into the kitchen and had a drink to get my eyes open. Then I took a shower and shaved. I got dressed, and this time I took my camera and my tape recorder with me. I went upstairs and knocked on Marya's door.

She opened it, looking as if she hadn't been up more than ten minutes.

"I'll meet you for breakfast," I said, "at the same place as yesterday. I'm sorry I couldn't make it last night, but I was busy until very late."

"I'll be right down, Peter," she said.

I went to the restaurant, and she came along in about fifteen minutes, looking fresh and lovely. We had breakfast together and then I dropped her off at her embassy, telling her I would make a special effort to see her that night. I drove on to the Automatic Machine Trust Building. When I reached my own office, I discovered there was somebody already there. It was Masinov.

"Comrade Miloff," he said formally, "I am Grigory Masinov. I have been assigned to be your security guard during the period that you are here serving the Soviet Union."

"I don't need a security guard," I said sourly. "I'm here to help build some machines and that's all."

"I have my orders, Comrade."

"All right. Make yourself comfortable and we'll see what goes on."

I sat down at the desk and brought out the blueprints, putting them in the desk drawer. The phone rang.

"*Slushayu. Kto govorit?*" I said when I picked up the phone.

"Am I speaking to Peter Miloff?" a man's voice asked. There was a strong accent to his Russian.

"Yes."

"I am Josip Voukelitch," he said. "I am a journalist from Yugoslavia. I have been informed of the work you are doing in the Soviet Union and I would like to do a story on it for my newspaper. I have already checked with the proper authorities and it has been approved—if you also agree."

"Let me call you back," I said. "Give me your phone number and I will call you within the hour."

I wrote down the number as he gave it to me and hung up. "I am going next door to see the director of this project," I said to Masinov. "I will soon be back." He nodded as I left the office.

I stopped in front of Ivanov's door, knocked lightly, and then opened it. He was alone, sitting behind his desk.

"May I speak to you for a few minutes?" I asked.

"Of course," he said jovially. "That is why I am here. Sit down, my dear Miloff."

I sat down. "There is a man in my office named Masinov who says he's been assigned as my security guard during my stay here."

"Oh, yes. While relations are presently very good between our countries, there may still be some hostility in parts of Russia and we thought it best to have someone around to protect you if you are ever threatened."

"That's very kind of you," I said gravely. "I don't think it's necessary, but I don't mind, if it's confined to my working hours. When it comes to whatever social life I may have, I don't want someone looking over my shoulder. I don't like being followed by the police at any time or anywhere, but I especially don't like it when it gets into the social side."

He smiled. "I understand. You seem to have had an active social life in the short time you have been here. I think I can promise you that the guard will not follow you when you have finished working."

"Thank you," I said. "I just received a call from a Yugoslavian journalist named Voukelitch. He wants to do a story on my work for his paper. I said that I would call him back."

"Good," he said, nodding. "You may tell him that he can do a story. He has already made an official request and it will be permitted. How was your first trip yesterday?"

"Fine. I'm going to go back to the same spots today and take photographs of them. You can have the film developed and the pictures enlarged, and they will be helpful in planning the places that certain machines are to be placed."

"An excellent idea."

"I will then make tape recordings on suggestions about the various locations.

Incidentally, were the places I saw yesterday fairly typical of spots where you plan on putting machines?"

"Yes. Is there something wrong with them?"

"No. They are fine locations, but I think you're missing a number of good spots. For example, factories and office buildings where the workers can get hot tea or food or cigarettes. I'd even put machines in places like prisons—for the use of the guards—and police stations, perhaps even military installations. Not only will it bring you a lot of money, but a lot of time will be saved. The work will be more efficient and less time will be wasted. Suppose a man runs out of cigarettes. Instead of going out on the street, he only has to walk a few feet to get them."

"That is an excellent suggestion," he said enthusiastically. "I will make up a list of such places for you to visit. Now, as soon as you feel like taking the time, we might also have a meeting on what is needed to start manufacturing the machines."

"That can start almost anytime," I told him. "I have blueprints of American machines and you can start making them at once, if you like. The only real change you will have to make in them is to alter the slot that accepts coins. You'll have to make that so it will accept your coins instead of ours. All the other parts are standard and easy to make."

"Good. I am very pleased with your efficiency, Miloff. You will leave the blueprints with me?"

"Before I go today."

He was beaming at me as I left. I walked back to my own office, where Masinov was patiently waiting. I picked up the phone and called *Pravda.* After a couple of minutes Irina came on the phone.

"Peter Miloff," I said. "How are you this morning?"

"I am wonderful, Peter," she said. "I was just about to call you. Where are you going today?"

"Back to the same places. I want to photograph them. If the pictures turn out good, maybe you can use them, too. Want me to pick you up, or do you want to come over here?"

"I'll be there soon."

"We're going to have company."

"What do you mean?"

"Well, I've been given a security guard so no one will beat me up, and there's a Yugoslavian journalist who wants to do a story on me, too."

She was silent for a second. "Fine," she said then, but her heart wasn't in it. "I'll see you in a few minutes, Peter."

Next I called Voukelitch and told him he could follow us around if he wanted to. He said he'd be over soon. I replaced the receiver and looked at Masinov.

"We'll have a parade," I said. "But I'd like to get one thing straight. I just spoke to Ivanov about it. I'll put up with a security guard during working hours, but when the day is over, I don't need a guard to take care of my social activities. Understood?"

"Understood. I am only following orders, you know."

"Sure," I said.

I took the blueprints from my desk and looked through them to make sure that I still remembered what they meant. They'd be turned over to engineers who probably could read them, but I wanted to be sure that I could answer any questions. By the time I'd finished checking them, Irina was there. I introduced her to Masinov. Then Voukelitch arrived. He turned out to be a big, blond man probably no more than thirty. He and Irina knew each other, so I only had to introduce him to Masinov.

It was almost a parade. Irina rode with me; Masinov and Voukelitch followed in their separate cars. We made the rounds of the same places I'd seen the day before, as I'd planned, and I photographed everything. We took a break for lunch. Irina and I ate together while Masinov and Voukelitch lunched at separate tables. We finished about four o'clock in the afternoon.

When we came out of the last place, I walked with Voukelitch to his car. Irina had already gotten into my car and Masinov was waiting in his.

"I'm sorry," I said to Voukelitch. "I didn't have much chance to talk to you today. If you want to come along tomorrow, I'll try to spend more time with you."

"Thank you," he said.

I took a deep breath and decided to get it over with. "Did you ever hear of Raskolnikov?"

He smiled. "I was just trying to get a chance to tell you that's my code name. And you're Uncle Vanya."

"So it seems," I said. "We'll try to talk about it later. But there are two things I want badly. I want to know where James Hartwell is and whether Richard Sorge is still alive. I'll see you tomorrow."

I turned and went back to my car.

"I have to go back to the office for a couple of minutes," I told Irina, "and then we can have a drink."

"All right," she said, "but Peter ..."

"Yes?"

"I can have a couple of drinks with you, but I can't spend the evening. I have to get some work done, and I'll be at the office until very late. I'm sorry."

"It's all right, honey. There's always tomorrow."

I drove back to the Automatic Machine Trust Building. Irina

stayed in the car while I went upstairs. I got the blueprints from my office and went to see Ivanov. I gave him the blueprints, then took the film from my camera and gave that to him too, before going back downstairs. Masinov was parked some distance behind my car. I went over to him.

"The working day is now over and the social day starts, so I will see you tomorrow. Maybe we'll get a chance to talk then."

He smiled. "We can talk now if we don't make it too long. There are no listening devices in my car and there is no one near us. What do you require?"

"Two things. Where is James Hartwell and is Richard Sorge still alive and running a special espionage bureau? Do you know anything about either of them?"

"No. I'll see what I can find out and tell you in the morning."

I nodded and went back to my car.

I followed Irina's directions and we ended up in a small but pleasant restaurant, where we had a couple of drinks. Then I drove her to *Pravda* and went back to my apartment. I made myself a drink and relaxed for a minute. I was not expecting very much from all of my little helpers, but I thought I might have something going for myself on Hartwell. At the moment I still didn't have a single idea about Sorge. I finished the drink, took a shower, and changed clothes. Then I went upstairs to knock on Marya's door.

She was home and obviously waiting for me. We went out and drove to the National Hotel, where we had dinner. There was no sign that we were being followed, and Masinov didn't show up in the dining room.

After dinner we drove around the city, stopping at various places for drinks. I had a deliberate plan, but tried to make it seem to be at random. We finally ended up at the little restaurant I knew, where we took a table. Nuritdin was there by himself. Zoubov was also there at another table. Nuritdin looked at me with a puzzled expression on his face. I could tell that he thought he knew me, but wasn't certain. It was several years since I had done business with him.

Our drinks were delivered and I took a sip. "I'll be right back," I told Marya.

I stood up and nodded at Nuritdin. Then I walked through the back of the restaurant. I remembered there was a rear door. I stepped outside and waited. A minute later Nuritdin joined me.

"You wanted to see me?" he asked.

"Yes. Do you remember me, Nuritdin?"

"I know I've seen you, but I don't remember exactly where."

"It was a few years ago.* This time I don't need to buy a car, but I want to sell some American dollars."

He struck his head with his open hand. "How could I forget? You almost ruined me. I was sick for a month." He stared at me for a second. "Are you running off with the wife of an important official again?" he asked sarcastically.

"Not yet," I said with a smile, "but I do have some American dollars to sell."

"How many?"

"One thousand dollars—at the moment. I may have more later."

---

* See *So Dead the Rose* by M.E. Chaber.

"You must print your own money," he said. "But as you are an old customer, I will give you a hundred and ten thousand rubles."

"You must be joking. I can get more than that from the government. I will be generous with you. I'll give them to you for a hundred and twenty thousand."

"You will put me out of business," he groaned. "I'll give you a hundred and fifteen thousand."

"All right," I said with a smile. "I'll take it." I pulled out some money and counted out a thousand dollars. In the meantime, he was also counting out money. We exchanged, and each of us counted what he had received.

"That's all?" he asked suspiciously.

I smiled. "For the moment. I may want something later."

"Don't rush."

"I won't, but don't talk—at least about meeting me before."

"I don't even talk to my wife," he said sourly. He went back into the restaurant.

I waited a minute and then followed him. Just as I reached the dining room, I stopped. As I'd thought, Georgi Zoubov was watching. I motioned with my head and went back outside. He showed up soon.

"You make out all right?" he asked.

"Sure. What about the gun?"

"I got it, but it'll cost you two hundred dollars. American money. That will include a box of ammo."

"Okay. Let me see it."

He pulled a gun from his pocket and handed it to me. It was a nickel-plated automatic.

"There is a full clip in it and the box of shells. The price is two hundred dollars in American money. That is what it costs me."

I tried the action of the gun. It worked smoothly. "Okay," I said. I gave him two hundred dollars. "Thanks. I'd better get back to the table. I don't know whether I'm being watched."

He nodded. "Cops are cops, no matter where you find them. As soon as you can, I want to talk to you. I have some business lined up for the Mob. You can take the idea back with you when you go."

"I'll try to get here one night soon. I'll have to make sure that I'm not followed."

"Yeah," he said. "I'll be here unless I get busted."

I put the gun and the box of shells in my pocket and went back to the dining room. Marya had almost finished her drink, so I called the waiter and ordered more.

We made two more stops after leaving there and then went to my apartment. I broke out the vodka and made drinks. She didn't ask me what I'd been doing and I didn't tell her. The first time she went to the bathroom, I put the gun away.

The next morning Marya and I had breakfast together and I dropped her off at the embassy, then went on to my office. Masinov was already there. I left my camera and went to see Ivanov. He had a big smile on his face as I came in.

"The photographs were wonderful," he exclaimed. "I can now see why you wanted to take them. The engineers are also very impressed; the blueprints are just what they need. We can get into production very soon."

"Good."

He picked up a sheet from his desk. "As to your suggestion of yesterday, it has been approved. Here is a complete list of Moscow factories, large business offices, and military establishments and prisons. We've listed only those that are large enough to make the plan practical. All of them will be notified that you are permitted to survey the premises, ask questions, and take photographs. I'm afraid that there is one condition."

"What's that?"

He seemed to be almost embarrassed. "You must understand, Miloff, it is not that we don't trust you, but in the case of the military and prison establishments we must ask you to turn the film over to your security guard as soon as you have shot it."

I shrugged. "I don't care whether I give it to you or to him."

"You are being most cooperative," he said. "I want you to know that we appreciate it. As a matter of fact, the way things are progressing, you may be able to go to Leningrad within a few days."

"All right. I told the *Pravda* journalist that she could probably use some of the photographs if they were good enough. I imagine they will talk to you about it. I'll see you tonight." I took the sheet of paper and went back to my own office.

I phoned Irina and she said she'd be right over. Next, I phoned Voukelitch, and he also said he'd come at once. I sat back to wait.

"They tell me," Masinov said, "that you're doing an excellent job."

"Why shouldn't I? It's what I was brought over here for."

"True. We must be paying you well for it, too."

"I haven't complained," I said. "If you're curious about how much I'm being paid, why don't you ask Comrade Ivanov?"

"I could find out," he said.

I couldn't tell whether he was talking for the benefit of the bug or was really throwing his weight around. I didn't much care.

"Be my guest," I told him.

Irina arrived first and Voukelitch came soon after. We all marched down the street and entered the three cars. Irina rode with me as before.

We made our rounds of factories, and I dutifully snapped pictures and explained to Irina and Voukelitch what sort of machines would be installed there. At the end of the day we went back to the Machine Trust and I turned my film over to Ivanov.

I had a chance to talk briefly with Voukelitch as we left. He had no information for me. I hadn't expected any. I had pretty much decided I couldn't expect, or trust, anything from them. I'd have to do it on my own.

Irina and I had a couple of drinks, but she had to work again that night, so I went home. Later I picked up Marya and took her to dinner.

The next day went by in much the same way. We covered office buildings and I took photographs. Sometime during the day I talked to all four of my helpers, but no one had any information. That night I went with Irina for a couple of drinks and then drove her to her office. She was going to work again. I drove home to keep a date with Marya.

The following day, it was military establishments. I was permitted to go where I wanted and to take the photographs. But I was watched every step of the way, and when I'd finished, I removed the film and gave it to Masinov.

Irina was working again that night and so was Marya. I went home and stayed there. I had a few drinks and fixed myself some dinner. For the first time I loaded microfilm into the camera.

It was a quiet evening. After dinner, I left the radio on and thought about my problems. I was hoping that I might get a chance to check on Hartwell when I visited the prisons. Irina would be with me and she knew what Hartwell looked like. If I could get a photograph of him, it would make it easier for our embassy to get to him. The big question was whether I would be able to get where I could see the prisoners. If not, I'd have to think of something else.

As for Sorge, I had no idea where to start. If he was still around, he'd probably be well under cover. I had no idea how to flush him out—unless he got interested in me.

That brought up another question, the message that I had gotten at the drop. It had not come through the regular channels, so my first feeling was to accept it as legitimate. But who was the bad apple in the barrel?

Irina? I didn't think so. There was something very sincere about her desire to go to America. Also, I thought, a point in her favor was that she wasn't a Russian agent, whereas the other three were.

Marya? I hadn't yet figured her out. She was actually a triple agent, which was dangerous in itself. But I had a feeling about her. I thought that she was caught up in something that made her completely vulnerable, and all she was doing at the moment was floating with the tide and trying to forget everything else.

I felt that Voukelitch wasn't really much of an agent for anyone. He was a nice guy, but I didn't think he was contributing very much.

Then there was Masinov. I was inclined to suspect him merely because he was in the KGB—which might be a mistake on my part. There was one other possibility. Who was Sasha, the agent who sent messages to everyone? He, or she, seemed even more likely.* The person who made all the drops was the most logical candidate. Sasha might be any one of the four or might be somebody else. As usual, I hadn't been given enough advance information.

I finally decided that I had to handle it in my usual way— play it by ear. I had another drink and went to sleep.

I was up early the next morning, showered, shaved, and got dressed. I had a small drink and some breakfast in the apartment. Then I drove to the office. By this time I had a large number of photographs, so I went over them and dictated remarks on the tape recorder. When I'd finished, I took the tape in to Ivanov. Masinov was in my office when I returned.

I phoned Irina and Voukelitch and said I'd be ready whenever they arrived.

Masinov and I exchanged small talk until they got there.

On the way to my car, I turned to Irina. "You met Hartwell. Would you recognize him if you saw him again?"

---

* The name Sasha can be either masculine or feminine, being a nickname for Aleksander or Aleksandra.

"I'm sure I would."

"All right. If we get a chance to see any prisoners today, you watch for Hartwell. If you recognize him, nudge me and indicate where he is."

"Yes, Peter."

The first prison was a small one. Accompanied by Irina, Masinov, and Voukelitch, I talked with the sergeant in charge and was permitted to take photographs.

"What about your prisoners?" I asked. "Do they have any money of their own that they can spend?"

He laughed. "Who ever heard of prisoners having money? Especially the ones we have here. They have been convicted of stealing a loaf of bread or some such thing."

I thanked him and left. The next prison was slightly larger, but not by much. They also had petty criminals only, and the sergeant said that they had no spending money.

The next stop was the Uzbekistan Prison. I knew that it was large and was used only for important, usually political prisoners. I photographed the rooms where we might place vending machines and took notes about the number of guards on duty at various times.

The director of the prison was there, and he and the sergeant both followed us around, asking me questions all the time. They were very excited about the entire project.

"Now," I finally said to the director, "do you have prisoners who are allowed to have their own money?"

"A few," he said. He sounded puzzled. "In some cases we allow them to give a guard money to buy something for them. It depends on the crime with which they are charged."

"It would be possible," I said, "for us to put one or two such vending machines inside the cellblock. Then the guard on duty could get things for them without leaving his post." I held my breath as I waited for his answer.

"I am not certain," he said, "that we should provide them with such luxuries."

I laughed. "I was not thinking of giving them luxuries. We would install one or two machines, depending on the prison population, but the products would not be as good as what would be available out here for you and your men. At the same time, the State would make all the profit and would have an accurate record of what the prisoners bought."

"That is true;" he said, but he was still hesitant. "Tell me, what would make the machines deliver their products?"

"Kopecks," I said. Then I had a sudden thought. "You understand that this is only a survey. It is possible that we will find it best to manufacture an artificial coin that will operate in these machines, and that such coins could be obtained only through your office. That would enable the director to keep a better watch on the money spent than if the prisoner gave money to a guard to go outside for him."

He nodded gravely, but I could see that he was already thinking this would enable him to make a little money on the side. "What do you need to do?" he asked.

"Just photograph the available space between the cells."

He made his decision. "We will go in," he said. He and the sergeant led the way to the locked door. The guard inside opened up and let us in. I made sure that Irina was beside me.

There were two tiers of cells on either side. I ignored

the cells as I lifted the camera and started taking pictures of the area in between. Then, suddenly, Irina nudged me. I glanced at her and saw she was looking up on the second tier. I followed her gaze and saw a thin, sandy-haired man watching us. He was certainly the one she was looking at. I pressed the concealed switch on the camera. Pretending to photograph other angles of the open space, I managed to point the camera in his direction and take several fast shots. I couldn't line the camera up on him, so I moved it around and hoped that one or more of the pictures would catch him. Then I switched back to the regular film and went on shooting.

I finished and we left. We covered four more prisons that afternoon and I went through the same procedure in each one. I turned all of the film over to Masinov when we stopped for the day.

Irina had dinner with me and we went back to her apartment. She went into the kitchen to make us drinks. While she was doing that I made another check of the apartment to see if it had been bugged since I was there before. It hadn't.

We were having our drinks and just beginning to relax when there was a knock on the door. She looked puzzled but got up and answered the knock. When she opened the door I heard the sound of a male voice. She turned around and her face was pale.

"It is for you, Peter," she said.

I stood up and looked at the man in the doorway. It was Masinov. "I'm sorry, Peter," he said, "but I have orders to escort you to the Kremlin."

NINE

There was a moment of silent melodrama. Masinov stood there with a noncommittal grin on his face. Irina looked as if she'd just been caught in a raid by the vice squad. I stared at Masinov and hoped that I looked undisturbed. Many things were going through my mind.

"All right," I said, "but it is rather late, isn't it?" Masinov had said the Kremlin, so I decided I wasn't being arrested and that it probably meant someone in the KGB was curious about me.

"True," he said, "but some of the comrades still have the habit of working at night. It is a hangover from the days of Stalin."

"Let's go, then," I said. I looked at Irina. "I'll see you later, baby."

I stepped out of the apartment and closed the door behind me. Masinov and I started walking down the corridor.

"What is all this?' I asked. "Don't tell me somebody wants me to build a vending machine that will produce instant girls."

He laughed. "I honestly do not know, Peter. The order came from my superior in the KGB. I am to escort you to an office in the Kremlin, but I do not even know who will be in that office. I am then to bring you back."

"That's encouraging," I said. "I'm glad that it's not like Chicago. How'd you know where to find me?"

"I think I could have guessed anyway, but it is known wherever your car is at any time."

So one of my guesses must have been right. There was a beeper on my car. They could follow me at a distance of several blocks and know when I stopped or where I went.

We reached the street and I looked at him. "We'll go in my car," he said. "I'll drive you back here."

We got into the car and drove away. Since we weren't too far from the Kremlin, we soon arrived. Masinov's credentials were examined by a guard, and we drove in and parked. I followed him upstairs in one of the buildings, and we walked down a long, empty corridor. As we passed the doors, I noticed that most of them bore names, either of individuals or bureaus. Finally we came to a door that looked different. The lettering on it said simply: *Chetyreh*. That is the Russian word for "four."

"This is where you go," Masinov said. "I will wait for you."

I looked at the door and then back at him. "There is no knob on the door. How do I get in?"

"You are expected. Just walk up and push on the panel."

I stepped forward. Just as I reached the door I heard a faint click and knew that it had been unlocked from inside or by a beam of invisible light. I pushed on the door—with my knuckles so there wouldn't be any fingerprints—and stepped inside. The door swung shut behind me without being touched.

It was a large office, the floor covered with a thick carpet.

There were several comfortable chairs scattered about and there were growing plants along one wall. Opposite me stood a partly open door. I had the feeling that it led to living quarters—I knew that there were such apartments in the Kremlin. But the center of attention in the office was a huge desk on the far side, with a map covering the entire wall behind it. The papers on the desk were neatly arranged. There was only the one soft light in the room, its rays directed over the desk but with most of the light concentrated on the chair in front of the desk.

A man was seated there. He was old, with completely white hair. His face was etched deeply with lines, but none of these were gentle lines. He looked detached and cold, as though it were a long time since he'd felt anything. He wore a nondescript gray suit that might have belonged to any man who wanted to fade into the background.

"Thank you for coming, Mr. Miloff," he said in English. "I am sorry to disturb you so late in the evening, but I find it more efficient to work at night. Won't you sit down?" He indicated the chair in front of his desk.

I sat down and looked at him. "I don't mind the hour, but I'm a little puzzled by everything else. Who are you?"

He smiled without warmth. "My name is completely unimportant. I am merely a small cog in the wheel of Russia. This is not, however, Mr. Miloff, a secret police questioning of you. I am interested in the work you are doing for our government. I have read reports that indicate that you are doing an excellent job. I am also told that you speak good Russian."

"Yes."

"Miloff is a Russian name?"

"Yes."

"And you are an American citizen?"

"Yes."

He tried that smile again with about the same result. "It is amusing, is it not? You are a Russian, but you are an American citizen! I am not a Russian, but I am a Russian citizen. Tell me, is it also true that you are an American gangster?"

"A lot of people think that all Americans are gangsters," I countered. "Maybe you've been seeing too many movies."

"I never see movies. The reports say that you are an American gangster from the city of Chicago."

"I'm from Chicago," I said coldly. "I work for the Brotherhood Coin Vending Company. It's a legitimate business."

"I know," he said. "But I am told that gangsters control much of the coin vending business in America. I am also told that the man who owns the company and for whom you work is a rather notorious gangster in that city. I am further told that you carried a gun regularly in America, even on your vacation, which you spent at an expensive home owned by the man you work for."

"So what?" I asked. "You knew all of that before you hired me, so why bring it up now?"

"I am a most curious man. I don't think that I have ever met an American gangster. But we will drop that if you are sensitive about it. I notice that you've had many social engagements since arriving in Moscow. First, there is Marya Rijekta, who works in the embassy of one of our allies. You find her interesting?"

"Yes."

"Then there is our own Irina Simonova, an excellent journalist who is doing a fine job of reporting our newest leap forward. I've seen advance copies of her first articles. But I also notice that you have spent some time in her company that was not devoted to business. In fact, you were in her apartment tonight when I wanted to see you. You also find her attractive?"

"Very."

"It is several years since I have been interested in women, but I can appreciate your good taste. I am interested only because while we have quite a few Americans visiting Moscow, for one reason or another we seldom find them leading as active a social life as you have. I believe you will spend very few evenings alone while you are here."

I decided it was time for me to take a more positive position. "I don't like it," I said. "I didn't ask to come here, and I didn't have any desire to come here. Someone from your country asked my company to suggest a man who could give you advice on coin machines. I was told that this would help international relations and I should accept the job. I did. But I didn't agree to do more than that. When I have finished what I am supposed to do, my time is my own, as long as I don't try to take over your country. And I can hardly take it over one woman at a time. So what I do at night is my business. Besides, I don't even know who you are or what you represent."

He shrugged.

"And," I continued, "how do you know that much about

what I do with my time? You must be bugging everything or having me tailed. Do you also have that nice apartment bugged?"

"Why do you ask that?"

"Because all cops think the same no matter where they come from. Bug and push. Well, I can't bug you back, but I can push back because I don't like to be pushed."

"I was just curious," he said mildly. "You interest me, Mr. Miloff. As I said, I've never met an American gangster before. But I have met many men who were similar to you in other ways. All right, we'll forget that. Would you like a cigarette?"

He pushed a beautiful box across the desk. It was made out of some kind of wood and would take perfect fingerprints.

"Thanks, but I'll smoke one of my own if you don't mind." I took a cigarette from my pocket and used my lighter. I was thinking about fingerprints, so I automatically dropped my hand in my lap and rubbed the lighter against my trousers. Then I noticed he was taking a cigarette from the box. I reached up and slid the lighter onto his desk.

"Here," I said, "here's another automatic machine we make in America. Try it."

He picked it up and lit his cigarette. He looked at the lighter curiously. "We make these, too."

"Not as good as that one," I said. "I'll make you a present of it." I held my breath, waiting for his reaction.

He turned it around in his hand, looking it over. "It is not as good as some of the ones we have," he said contemptuously. He slid it back across the desk, and I picked it up carefully and dropped it in my pocket.

"Would you like a drink?" he asked.

"No, thanks."

He sighed. "All right. I know that the Automatic Machine Trust is very pleased with the work you've done so far. Tell me, what kind of machines are you helping us to build?"

"They must have told you that, too. The machines will dispense such things as food items, hot tea, milk, candy, and cigarettes. They can also be built to dispense vodka or almost anything else you want. My advice does not go as far as telling you what to sell. Your Machine Trust will tell me what you want to sell, and I will tell them how to build the machine and where to place it."

"You think this will mean progress for the Soviet Union?"

"I haven't thought about it. I wasn't hired to give advice on your progress. It's merely something that you people decided you wanted. I was hired to tell you how to get it. That's all there is to it—and all there will be."

He nodded and stared at me with eyes that were dull from age—and maybe from seeing too much. "I have the list of places you've been visiting and photographing—public stores, in some cases, streets, factories, office buildings, military establishments, and prisons. You are, I understand, going to go through the same schedule in other Soviet cities. Why?"

"First, by looking at the places I can get an idea of what sort of people frequent them. That will in turn give me an idea about what should be sold in those spots. All of this is covered in the reports that I dictated. The photographs enable me to advise the engineers on the best locations for the machines."

"What about the military locations? Did your advice cover them?"

"Yes."

"Why?"

"For the same reason as at other places. It will result in less loss of manpower, and less time away from duty, while the government also makes all the profit from what people spend."

"And what did you photograph at the military locations?"

"The same things I photographed everywhere else, the spots where it would be best to place machines." I smiled at him. "You can be sure I was well watched and that every piece of film was turned over to the security guard before we left."

"So I have been informed. What about the prisons? Why did you suggest them?"

"The same reason." I made myself begin to sound exasperated. "Less time off on the part of guards or other prison employees. In prisons, where some of the inmates are allowed to have money, I suggested that machines be put in between the cellblocks."

"Why can't money be spent in the same machines the guards use?"

"I thought that the machines for the prisoners would not offer the same choice or the same quality as the others. Also, the guard on duty inside would not have to leave his section to get something for a prisoner."

"And the photographs?"

"The film was turned over to the security guard before we left each prison."

He stared at me, his fingers drumming on the desk. "Well," he said slowly, "the Machine Trust is very pleased with what you are doing. Everybody is happy—except me."

"You don't approve of your country installing the vending machines?"

"Frankly, I don't think it means anything one way or the other. It is not the machines which interest me; it is you."

"I am flattered. But I still don't know who or what you are. Tomorrow, I may find myself in trouble with some established authority here because I've even talked to you. Just who do you represent?"

"The Soviet Union," he snapped. "That is all you need to know."

"That's cop talk, so you must be a cop. What interests you about me—the girls?"

"Not just girls, but I am interested in why you picked those two particular women."

"Your facts are a little off," I said. "You'd better shake up your boys. I met Miss Rijekta by accident in a restaurant the first night I was here. We discovered that we lived in the same building, and I have seen her several times since then. I met Miss Simonova because she was assigned by her newspaper to do a series of articles on my work. You can't make much out of that."

He stared at me glumly. "Yes, everything seems very correct, doesn't it? The only thing that bothers me is you."

"Why do I bother you? Am I wearing the wrong sort of tie?"

"As far as I know," he said, "I have a fairly good idea what American gangsters are like. You do not fit the picture. You are obviously educated. You are able to plan and set up a complicated business. I doubt if there are many gangsters like that. On the other hand, you seem very sure of yourself, and there is steel inside of you. I suppose that there are gangsters like that. But it also fits other sorts of people I know or have known. And then there are Marya and Irina."

I smiled. "It seems to me that you are more bothered by my social activities than anything else. But it's not too different from men of every country, no matter what they do for a living. I don't imagine taking girls out is a crime even here."

"Mr. Miloff, have you ever known a man named Georgi or George Zoubov?"

I pretended to think. "I never knew him, but I've heard of him. He used to be with the Mob in Chicago. I think I heard that he came to Russia or was deported—something of the sort."

"He's living here now, although I understand that he is not especially happy about it. He knows only one profession, and the Soviet Union does not approve of crime."

"Neither does the United States," I said with a smile.

He sighed heavily. "Well, Mr. Miloff, you may go, if you're sure you don't want a drink." He looked at me questioningly, then he went on. "But I should warn you that I shall continue to be interested in you. I hope you will also remember an old Russian proverb." For the first time he switched to Russian. *"Ti n'yeh znahyesh, shtoh chelovyek sohstohit iz t'yehlah, dushi i pahsportah?"* It meant, "You don't know that a man is made up of his body, his soul, and his passport?"

"I've heard of it. You can't take away my passport—so is that meant as a threat?"

"No—just a reminder. Good night, Mr. Miloff."

I got up and walked back across to the door. It didn't open, so I stopped.

"There is a button to the left of the door," he said. "All you have to do is press it and the door will open." I reached out and pressed the button with the knuckle of my forefinger. The door swung open. I started to step through.

"Mr. Miloff," he said from behind me.

I turned to look at him. "Yes?"

"I have noticed that you are a most cautious man. It makes me even more curious. I will see you again soon. Good night."

I stepped into the corridor and the door closed behind me.

TEN

Grigory Masinov was waiting in the corridor for me. We walked downstairs and out to his car. Neither one of us said anything as we drove off. He had to show his identification again before we could leave.

"What did he want?" Masinov asked after we'd gone about a block.

"To talk about the work I'm doing here. Now you tell me something. Who is he?"

"He didn't tell you?" he asked. He sounded surprised. "I don't know who you saw, Peter. My orders were merely to escort you to that room. I've never been there before. But he must be someone important. Do you think he suspected you?"

"I don't think so." That wasn't exactly true, but I had decided to play everything close to my chest. "He asked a lot of questions about the vending machines. I got the impression that he didn't care too much for that type of progress."

"Young or old?"

"At least seventy."

"Then he must be a member of the old guard. A lot of them want to go back to former times."

We drove until we reached the building where Irina lived. I got out of the car.

"Thanks for the ride, Grigory," I said. "Now I'll go back to my social life and you can go do the same. Only tell me one thing before you leave. Who is Sasha?"

He looked at me blankly. "I don't know. My only contact with him has been through messages left at the drop in the park."

"Him? Are you sure it's a man?"

"No. I just thought it was from the name. I guess it could be a woman."

"All right. I'll see you in the morning."

I turned and entered the building. When I reached her door, I took out my handkerchief and wiped off the door-knob. I had probably left my prints on it. Then I knocked on the door.

Irina still looked frightened when she opened the door. I stepped inside and, as I closed the door behind me, rubbed my handkerchief over the knob. Then I took her in my arms. Her whole body was trembling.

"It's all right, honey," I told her. "It was nothing to be frightened about."

"What did they want?" she asked.

"Just to ask me questions about the vending machines, that was all."

"Who was it? The KGB?"

"I don't know who it was. He was a very old man who didn't tell me his name. I got the impression that he didn't approve of all this mechanical progress. There's nothing to worry about." I kissed her.

She calmed down. "I'm sorry, Peter. I was so worried about you. I was afraid you wouldn't come back."

"I'm here," I said. "Make me a drink and don't worry anymore."

She went into the kitchen and I sat down on the couch. I took out a cigarette and started to reach for my lighter, then I remembered. I looked around and spotted some matches, picked them up, and lit my cigarette. Then I slipped the matches into my pocket and concentrated on my immediate problem, while the pleasant sound of ice and liquids came from the kitchen.

Irina came in with two drinks. She put them on the small table and sat down next to me. She leaned over and kissed me on the cheek.

"I'm happy that you're back," she said.

"I'm happy to be back," I answered. I took a sip from the drink. "It's not very late. Do you think I could still get into the building of the Machine Trust?"

She looked at her watch. "There should be people working there and you have identification, so you shouldn't have any trouble getting into your office. Why?"

"Just to play it safe, I should pick up the tape recorder and catch up on my dictation. That man who wanted to talk to me is following all of the records, including the advance proofs of your articles. I haven't kept up to date, so I'd better get everything in tomorrow morning."

She looked unhappy. "You mean you're going to leave right away?"

"I think I'd better, honey," I said. "I'd much rather stay here, but it'll be best for both of us if I catch up on my homework. Don't let it bother you, honey. We'll have plenty of time to see each other. In fact, I think we're going to Leningrad in a day or two, sooner than I'd expected."

"What makes you think I'll go?" she asked.

"I'll request it. I'm sure you will. You'll love Leningrad."

"You forget," she said dryly, "that I'm a Russian and you are not. I've been to Leningrad."

"Not until you've been there with me," I said with a smile. I finished my drink and put the glass down. "Do me one favor, honey."

"What?"

"As soon as I leave, will you take this glass and wash it very carefully?"

"Why?"

"For the moment let us just say that I like to see a woman be a tidy housekeeper. I'll explain it more fully later on."

"All right, Peter."

"Good girl." I stood up and held out my arms. "Give me a kiss and then let me out."

She kissed me and almost changed my mind, but I still made it to the front door. I kissed her once more after she'd opened the door, then fled down the corridor.

I drove to the Machine Trust Building and parked, entered the building, and immediately encountered a guard. I had to show him my card before he escorted me up to my office. I produced a key for it, and that seemed to satisfy him. He left as I went inside.

First I took the microfilm from the camera. I carefully removed any traces of fingerprints from the camera and went over everything else in the room. Then I picked up the tape recorder and left. I drove straight back to my apartment.

I looked the apartment over carefully, but there was no indication that anyone had been there. I made myself a drink and turned on the radio. Then I quickly went over the apartment, trying to erase every spot where I might have left fingerprints, before going back to my drink. I turned off the radio and started dictating to the tape recorder—knowing that every word was also being picked up by the hidden microphone.

The telephone rang after I had been dictating for about fifteen minutes. I was startled. It was the first time it had rung since I'd been there. I shut off the tape recorder and picked up the receiver.

"Who is speaking?" I asked.

"Peter," she said, "this is Marya. I wasn't sure that you would be home, but I thought I'd try."

"Where are you?" I asked.

"I'm still at the embassy, but I've almost finished my work and I thought you might like to take me to dinner."

"I'd love to," I said. "Why don't you meet me in the bar of the National Hotel when you're finished? I'll probably be there before you are. If not, wait for me. Otherwise I'll wait for you."

"All right, Peter," she said. She sounded happy. "I'll see you very soon." She hung up.

I dictated a few more sentences, then cut the tape recorder off and turned the radio on again. I took a fast shower and dressed, making sure that my gun was well hidden. Then I washed the glass I'd been drinking from and wiped off the telephone and the tape recorder. As I left the apartment I also rubbed the knob on both side of the door.

I was positive that the white-haired man had made two attempts, maybe three, to get my fingerprints. One had been the cigarette box and the other was the button to open the door. The offer of a drink may have been the third attempt. I felt that sometime soon, maybe that night, men would check my office and the apartment. The absence of prints would be very suspicious—but it wouldn't be as bad as if they found my prints. The KGB had the fingerprints of Milo March, and I didn't want them to have a chance to find out that mine matched the ones they had on file.

I got in the car and drove to the National Hotel, parked, and went inside. I finished the drink I ordered, and the bartender came over to see if I wanted another.

"I'm meeting a young lady here," I told him, "but I remembered I must make a couple of phone calls. I'll be right back."

He nodded and I went out to the lobby. I picked a new exit. I was pretty certain that there wasn't a tail on me except for the beeper on the car, but I wasn't taking any chances. Outside of the hotel I quickly found a taxi. I told him to take me to a spot that was about a block away from the restaurant I wanted. I gave him ten rubles and asked him to wait for me when we'd arrived.

At the restaurant, I was in luck. Nuritdin was standing in front, looking as glum as usual.

"How about a walk?" I asked.

He looked up and down the street. "All right," he said. We walked in leisurely fashion along the street. "You're bad news," he said. "I remembered everything from the time I saw you years ago. Whose wife do you want to spend a few days with now?"

"You made a profit, didn't you?"

"Yes. But I was sick for weeks. What do you want? More rubles?"

"Yes—for one thing."

"How much?"

"A thousand dollars."

"I can give you that much now. I just happen to have it with me."

He sounded relieved as he dug into his pocket and we exchanged the money.

"Now," I said, "I want something else."

"I was afraid of that. What?"

"I want a passport and a visa."

"Russian?"

"No. American passport. Russian visa."

"That is not easy," he said slowly. "I'm not saying that it's impossible, but it is difficult. It will be expensive."

We rounded the corner into a completely empty street. "I didn't say anything about how much it would cost," I said mildly. "I want the papers by tomorrow night. I'll pay whatever it costs—in American dollars. Do you want to make notes or can you remember?"

"I can remember."

"I'll give you the passport that I am currently carrying. It has my photograph. Make a copy of it. I may still need this one for a while. But don't use the same name on the new passport. Put in the name of Milo March." I spelled it for him so that he'd be sure to get it right.

"I understand. But what you ask for will cost a good deal.

It means using a fine artist and making him rush something that should take several days."

"How much?"

"Two thousand American dollars."

"It is too much," I told him, "but I will pay it to you this once. I must, however, have the papers early tomorrow night. I am not sure when I will have to leave Moscow."

"In advance," he said.

I shook my head. "I'll give you five hundred in advance and the rest when I get the papers."

He shrugged. "All right. You drive a hard bargain, comrade."

I counted out five hundred dollars and handed it to him. "I'll see you at the restaurant early tomorrow night." I turned and walked back, looked inside the restaurant, and spotted Georgi Zoubov sitting alone at one of the tables. I went in and ordered a drink. I finished it quickly and put money on the table as I caught Zoubov's gaze. I motioned with my head and walked out again, headed up the street.

A moment later I heard steps behind me. I slowed up to let him overtake me.

"Hi, pal," he said as he fell into step with me. "How's it going?"

"I'm not so sure. I'm being tailed, but at the moment they think I'm at the National Hotel. I don't have much time. You said you wanted to talk to me about something."

"If you're crowded for time, we can make it another night."

"I'm not so sure of that. I think I'll be leaving Moscow either tomorrow night or the day after."

"Back to Chi?"

"Not yet. Leningrad. I don't know if I'll be back in Moscow or not. So you'd better tell me now—quickly."

"Okay. When you get back to the big town, you tell Angelo Benotti that I have a whole setup for regular large shipments of heroin. Good stuff, already processed, and the price is good."

I was surprised. I didn't think there was any opium in the Soviet Union. "From here?" I asked.

"No. I made a contact with a Chink who's here with the Red China trade commission. They've set up processing plants there and can deliver the heroin directly."

"Why through you? I thought they had a number of routes for taking opium out of the country. The same routes should do just as well for heroin."

"I guess they just want a new way. They'll deliver the stuff to me here in Moscow. I've already set up a way to get it from here to Bucharest, Romania. There's enough traffic in and out of there so that pickups can be made easily."

Suddenly I was very interested. I was glad I had taken the time to talk to him again. It sounded to me like something that would interest the men back in Washington. Maybe the Chinese wanted to develop a new route and maybe they had a little double-cross in mind, since things were going so badly between them and Russia.

"How do you know your contact can deliver? Who is he?"

"His name is Chen Huang, and he's a regular member of the trade commission.

He's already brought me a sample—pure stuff."

"How are you going to get it out?"

"Through a Romanian pilot who makes regular flights between Bucharest and Moscow. It's a beautiful setup."

"How do we pick it up?"

"There's a guy in Bucharest named Lazarus. He runs a shop at the airport, makes a lot of sales to Americans who either carry the stuff out or ship it out—things like statues, replicas of old buildings and churches, and souvenirs of all kinds. The H will be placed inside these items and sealed, so that they'll have to be broken to get it out. Tell Benotti that the price is thirty percent under European prices."

"Okay," I told him. "I'll deliver the message when I get back. If I do return to Moscow, I'll talk to you again. How soon can you make a delivery after you get the okay?"

"Two weeks. After that, deliveries can be made once a month. Fifty pounds of pure H each time. Later, we can increase it."

"Sounds good. Two more questions. How do we get in touch with you to tell you to go ahead?"

"The boys know. I just get a letter from my Uncle Alexander in Chicago. He's been dead two years, but they don't know that here. Just start the first sentence with "Yes," and two weeks later it'll be in Bucharest."

"How will the man in Bucharest know that he's dealing with the right guy?"

"Just say that Zoubov sent you."

"Okay. I'll see you, pal," I said.

I turned back and hurried to where I'd left the taxi. It was still there. I had the driver take me back to the same hotel entrance where he'd picked me up, and gave him a large tip before I went inside.

Marya was sitting at the bar, a drink in front of her. I slipped onto the next stool and motioned to the bartender.

"Been waiting long?" I asked.

"Only about ten minutes. Where were you?"

"Making some phone calls. I'm sorry I kept you waiting."

The bartender brought me a drink and went away. "It's all right, Peter," she said. "I hope you didn't mind that I called you."

"I was glad, Marya."

"I just wanted to see you," she continued. She sounded very nervous.

"Anything wrong?"

"Nothing new," she said sorrowfully.

We had a few more drinks at the bar and I noticed she was beginning to feel them. Then we went into the dining room and had dinner. We had some brandy after dinner and went out to the car.

When we got back to our building, she put her hand on my arm. "Peter," she said, "could we go sit in the park for a few minutes?"

"Of course," I said.

We got out of the car and walked to the park. It was still early enough so that there were a few people there, but we found a bench away from the others.

"Marya," I said, "who is Sasha?"

She looked at me with a startled expression. I knew it was because she was lost in her own thoughts. "Sasha?" she said. "He's the one I get messages from at the drop."

"Yes, but do you have any idea who he—or she—is?"

"No. The messages are the only contact I've ever had with Sasha."

"All right, honey. I thought you might have a clue. You don't, so forget it."

From the way she looked, I knew she already had. She sat there, staring off at the stars in the sky. She was a little bit drunk and she was shivering, but I knew it was not caused by either the drink or the weather. I put my arm around her shoulders.

"Peter," she said in a very low voice, "do you suppose it's safe to talk here?"

"I imagine so," I said. "They can't really wire every bench in every park."

"I don't know if I can go on any longer. I just don't know. It's all so horrible."

I knew that it was not the time for me to say anything, so I only held her tight and waited.

"You've been nice to me, Peter. Nicer than anyone I've known in a long time. Not like the others."

"What others?" I asked gently.

She suddenly gripped my hand. "Do you know what I am, Peter?"

"Sure. You're a very lovely girl. And you're also a triple agent—which is enough to make anyone a little nervous."

I don't think she even heard me.

"I'm nothing but a prostitute, did you know that, Peter? All I'm supposed to do as an agent is to go to bed with men and listen to what they have to say. My own people want me to go to bed with Russians and report what they say. The Russians want me to go to bed with all sorts of men and report what they say. And then all the beds have a microphone somewhere near them and some dirty little man is sitting somewhere and listening to all that goes on. I was even ordered to go to bed with you. Did you know that?"

"I didn't know it, but I suspected it. It's all right, Marya."

She shook her head. "It's not all right. And it wasn't like that when I did go to bed with you. It was different. I didn't remember to try to get information out of you, and I even forgot the microphone for a while. Did you know that?"

"I think I did, Marya. I forgot about those things, too. … Who gave you your orders?"

"The Russians. I've had to make reports every day after I've seen you. But I've never told them anything about you except that you keep talking about those machines. That's really all. You have to believe me."

"I do believe you, honey. What about us, the Americans? Do we order you to go to bed with people, too?"

"No, but I'm sure that they must have known that was all I was good for when they hired me. So I go to bed with the Russians and I tell my country and your country, and I go to bed with other men and I tell the Russians, my country, and your country. That's all I do. Go to bed and make reports about it. One day—soon—I will be too old to go to bed with anyone, and then no one will want anything to do with me."

I squeezed her shoulder. "It'll be a long time before you're that old, Marya. Let's go upstairs and I'll make a drink for you."

She turned to look at me. "Do you mean that you still want me to come to your apartment after what I've just told you?"

"Of course I do."

"Oh, Peter," she said, twisting into my arms and starting to cry.

I held her close. "Marya," I said, "it's a tough world, the one you chose to live in. I've lived in it long enough to know. You can't always use the same rules that the rest of the world goes by. Things happen to us that the rest of the world doesn't even believe when they read about it. You have to develop a layer of toughness that doesn't let everything get through to you. But don't let the toughness get all the way inside. Now, let's dry up those tears." I took my handkerchief and wiped the moisture from her face. "Come on and I'll make that drink for you."

We stood up.

She lifted her face and kissed me. "Thank you, Peter. Do you think I can ever come to America?"

"Of course, you can. All you really have to do is go to the American Embassy and ask for political asylum. When you get to America you can write a book about your experiences and that'll probably make you rich."

She laughed. "I'd like that. Make me the drink, Peter." I kept my arm around her as we walked back to the building and went up to my apartment. I looked around as we entered, but I couldn't see any sign that someone had been there. I turned on the radio, and Marya sat down while I went into the kitchen and made two drinks.

We sat and talked and drank. Most of the talk was about her country and her childhood, and it was all safe. She was still drinking faster than I'd ever seen her do before, and it wasn't long until her speech became slurred. Still, the minute she'd finish a drink she'd push the glass to me to be refilled.

She was getting very drunk, and I was a little worried that she might say the wrong thing, but she didn't. She finally picked up a drink I had just brought her, drank about half of it at one gulp, then carefully set the glass down on the table. She looked at me and said, "Oh, Peter!" Then' she fell against me and was unconscious.

I picked her up and carried her into the bedroom, undressed her, and put her to bed. I went back to the other room, closing the bedroom door, and made myself a fresh drink. Then I started dictating where I had stopped when she'd phoned. It took me about an hour to finish. I went to bed and found Marya sleeping in the same position as when I'd left her.

She was still sleeping when I awakened the next morning. I took a quick shower and shaved, then went into the kitchen and put on some coffee. That was one of the things I'd managed to buy the day I'd shopped. I didn't have all the ingredients, but I made a couple of imitation Bloody Marys and carried them into the bedroom. By the time I was dressed, Marya was beginning to stir.

She awakened slowly. First she opened her eyes just enough to see through the parted lids. As always, the first place she looked was at the light that held the microphone. Next she looked around the room until she found me. Only then did the fear leave her face and her eyes open all the way.

"Oh, Peter," she said, "I feel terrible."

"Sure you do, honey." I carried a Bloody Mary over to her. "Drink this and it will make you feel a little better."

She obediently took a sip of it. "I'm sorry, Peter. I had too much last night."

"I think that sums it up accurately," I said gravely.

"I am sorry. Did—did I say anything terrible to you?" I knew she was worried about spilling something.

"No," I said. "You were perfectly fine." I felt like a character in a Dorothy Parker story.*

She looked relieved. "Did you put me to bed?"

"Yes. Now I'm your doctor. Drink that and we'll have made a start in getting you to feel better."

She took a long drink. "It is very good. Will it really make me feel better?"

"Guaranteed."

We both finished our drinks.

"Now," I said, "take a good long shower and then come into the kitchen."

I pulled back the covers and gave her a light smack on the bottom. I picked up the glasses and went to the kitchen. The coffee was just about ready. I had some buns I'd bought and also smoked fish, which I knew she liked. I put those on the table plus plates and cups and utensils. Then I made myself another drink.

Later she came into the kitchen. She had just come from the shower and was naked. There were still a few drops of water on her body, and her hair was damp.

"I feel better already," she said. "Am I pretty, Peter?"

"Beautiful," I said. "And the rest of the prescription is now ready."

---

* "You Were Perfectly Fine" was a 1929 short story by Dorothy Parker, one of America's great humorists, in which a young man tries to find out what he did the night before while he was very drunk at a party.

She looked at the table. "Oh, you made breakfast!"

"Well, I didn't exactly make it," I said modestly. "I merely bought it. Although I did make the coffee."

"May I have breakfast without getting dressed?"

"Sure. I may have a little trouble concentrating on my food, but it'll be a pleasure."

The Bloody Mary must have done the job, for she ate breakfast with enthusiasm. Afterwards she got dressed. I was ready to leave by the time she was headed up to her apartment to change clothes.

I decided the corridor was relatively safe. "If you feel like it," I said, "call me at the Machine Trust this afternoon. I may be going to Leningrad either late tonight or sometime tomorrow. But maybe we can at least have dinner together tonight."

"You're darling, Peter," she said. "I will call you." She ran up the stairs and I went down to my car.

Masinov was sitting in my office when I entered. Everything else looked pretty much the same, but I had a feeling that someone had gone through the place. I was positive when I sat down at the desk and noticed a trace of what looked like fingerprint powder on one drawer.

"You fooled me last night," Masinov said. I couldn't tell by his tone whether he was chiding me or kidding.

"How did I fool you?"

"You didn't stay at the apartment where I left you, but came back here to the office."

"I didn't tell you that I was going to stay there, so I didn't fool you. When the day is over, what I do is my business. I was told that the reason you're assigned to me is to protect me from the people. I don't think I need it."

"I don't make the rules," he said with a smile. "You came back here to get your tape recorder. Why?"

"I had work to do, which I did last night in my apartment." I opened the recorder and took out the tape. "This is it. Would you mind taking it in to Ivanov?"

"I don't mind," he said.

I handed it to him, being careful not to touch it anywhere that a print could be taken. "And tell him I'll be in to see him very shortly, if it's convenient."

He nodded and left with the tape. As soon as he was out of the office, I used my handkerchief to go over the tape recorder. I didn't know if they'd try to check it while I was with Ivanov, but I wasn't going to take any chances. Then I used the same handkerchief to open a drawer and remove some notes I had made. I glanced at them briefly and then stepped away from the desk and waited, watching the door. When I saw the shadow on the other side of the frosted glass, I walked toward the door. I was almost at it when Masinov opened it.

"I'm going to see him now," I said, and stepped past him, leaving him to close the door. I walked down the corridor and knocked at Ivanov's door. His voice told me to come in. I palmed the knob so that my fingers wouldn't touch it, and opened the door. I realized that a complete absence of fingerprints would be suspicious and dangerous, but not nearly as dangerous as giving them definite samples of my prints. After I stepped into the office, I closed the door with my elbow.

"Ah, there you are Miloff," Ivanov said. "I didn't expect you so soon. Masinov just brought in the tape."

"I had intended to come in after I'd done some work, but I just went over my notes and realized I had more to do than I'd thought. If this is an inconvenient time, I can come back later."

"No, no. This is fine. Sit down."

I took the chair next to his desk. "I have checked over my notes. I have about two hours of dictation to do and that should finish up the present plans for Moscow. There may be other spots that we might want to consider later when I return here. But I think we can finish this stage today and then I can go anywhere you wish me to go. On the other hand, if you want to cover other spots here first, then we'll do that. You are paying me and I will do whatever you want. I'm just reporting."

He chuckled. "Of course. I know that. As a matter of fact, you are right. We have already decided that you will leave for Leningrad tomorrow morning—at eight o'clock. You may drive to the airport and the car will be picked up there. That will give you plenty of time to finish your dictating and get ready to leave." He smiled. "And to get your social affairs adjusted to your absence for a time."

I smiled back. "That is very considerate of you. When I return, will I move back into the same apartment?"

"I imagine so. But why do you ask?"

"I wanted to know whether I should take all of my luggage or leave some of it in the apartment."

He pursed his lips. "I'm not sure of your exact itinerary after Leningrad. Perhaps it would be best to take all of your luggage with you. You will be going to other cities and you may need your things. However, I leave that up to you. Incidentally, you will be accompanied by Comrade Masinov, who will continue to act as your security guard."

"That's fine. I don't think it is necessary, but I find him most efficient."

"This should please you," he said with another smile. "You will also be accompanied by Comrade Simonova. It has been decided that she will continue the series of articles and cover every city you visit. In the meantime, here we will be working on the problems of getting into production."

"May I make a suggestion?"

"Certainly. Please do. That is why we obtained your services."

"I have considered all the problems," I said, "and it seems to me that you will need machines that will fall into one of four categories of machine. You might save considerable time and money by ordering one each of those four machines from Chicago. They could be dismantled and gone over by your engineers. Some of the parts might be pieces which you already make or which would need only a slight modification. With the others you could take a mold that would shorten the process of making master dies."

He looked thoughtful. "Yes, that might be an advantage. Did you include that suggestion in your latest report?"

"No. I thought I would leave that up to you."

He liked that. It meant he could take the credit. "There might be a problem in getting the machines quickly. I'm not even sure they are on the list of things we can import from your country."

"I don't think there should be any problem," I said. "Our State Department gave its consent to this project. If I may, I suggest that you put through a regular request to purchase the machines. I will give you the numbers of the four. Then, with your permission, I will send a message to my company, telling them to send you the machines by air freight at once, and I will go to my embassy and impress them with the fact that they should get in touch with the State Department in Washington and urge them to see that the order goes through quickly."

He thought for a moment. I could see him weighing the advantages to himself. "You think they will do it?"

"I'm positive they will," I said. "We are in a period of better relations between our two countries, and they will want to do it once it is brought to their attention."

"I think you are right," he said, nodding his head. "You will do that for us?"

"Yes."

"Good. Then I give my approval." He hesitated a minute. "You may find some of our people suspicious of you, Miloff, but I would like to tell you that the Machine Trust feels that you are doing much more for us than we expected, and we would be proud to think of you as a comrade. You may take the two steps you suggested."

"Thank you, Comrade Ivanov," I said.

He smiled and reached out to shake my hand. "I will put through a formal order for the four machines. What are the numbers?"

"I'll give them to you when I bring in the next tape. That

will be soon. It will give you enough time to clear the placing of an order."

I stood up and left, palming the doorknob again so there wouldn't be any prints on it.

Masinov was still sitting in my office. "I hear," he said as I came in, "that we're going to Leningrad."

"So I was just told," I answered. "At eight o'clock in the morning. A terrible hour. Tell me, do they serve vodka on the planes?"

"I believe so."

"That's encouraging. I have to do some work now. Be a good fellow and answer the phone if it rings. Tell me who it is and I'll decide if I want to talk to them or not."

He nodded.

I took out a fresh tape and put it in the recorder. Using my notes, I began to cover everything that hadn't been in the previous recordings. It was a bore, but I tried to sound enthusiastic.

The phone rang and Masinov answered. He covered the mouthpiece and said, "It's Voukelitch."

"Tell him I'll call him later. And get his number. I don't have it."

He moved his head to indicate he understood, and I could hear him talking as I continued dictating. I was almost through when the phone rang again. Masinov answered and again covered the mouthpiece. "It is Comrade Simonova," he said.

"Okay," I told him. He handed me the phone and I took it, still being careful about fingerprints. "Hello, Irina," I said. "You're up late this morning."

"I've already been working several hours," she said. There was a peculiar quality to her voice, as though she were under some strain. "I've been assigned to cover your trip to Leningrad."

"That's fine," I said. "It should be a good series. I believe that I'll also go to other cities and eventually come back here."

"I don't know if I will go on beyond Leningrad. But I called to tell you that I'll have to work late tonight in order to make the plane in the morning. I would like to get some advance information from you. Perhaps we could meet for a drink when you are ready?"

"I have a better idea," I said. "I'm almost finished here now. I still have a few things to do this afternoon, but why don't we meet for lunch? Say in an hour?"

"All right," she said. She sounded slightly relieved. "Where?"

"National Hotel?"

"Good. I will meet you there in an hour. Good-bye, Peter."

I hung up and went back to work. But there was still another phone call. This time it was Marya.

"Peter," she said. She sounded almost the same as she had in the park the night before. "Am I going to see you tonight?"

"Sure, honey. I'm not positive what time I'll get home, but it should be early. Why not call me there or just come and meet me and we'll go out for dinner?"

"All right, Peter." She hung up.

"Do all Americans," Masinov asked as I replaced the receiver, "have so much social activity?"

"They try to," I told him with a smile. "Some succeed and some don't."

I went back to dictating and was finished in thirty minutes. Then I took the tape out of the machine, and on a sheet of paper wrote the numbers of four vending machines that the Chicago company sold.

"Comrade Masinov," I said, "would you do me a favor and deliver these to Comrade Ivanov? By the time you return I will be ready to leave."

"Of course," he said. He picked up the tape and the sheet of paper and left.

As soon as he was gone, I got busy making certain I had not left any prints on anything. I had finished and was just sitting at the desk, smoking a cigarette, when Masinov came back.

"Comrade Masinov," I said, "I don't imagine I'll be back at the office today, so I'm taking the camera, the tape recorder, and my notes with me. Would you be so kind as to look them over and make certain that I am not removing anything that belongs to the Soviet Union?"

There was a puzzled expression on his face as he looked at me, but he came over and examined everything. "It's all in order," he said.

"Thank you," I replied. I picked up the papers and put them in my pocket. Then I took the camera in one hand and the tape recorder in the other. "Let's go."

He opened the door and I stepped out into the corridor, waiting until he joined me. "I'd better stop for a final word with Comrade Ivanov," I said.

We reached Ivanov's office and I nodded at Masinov, who knocked on the door, then opened it.

"Ah, Comrade Miloff," Ivanov said as he looked up. "I

have just put through the formal purchase order on those machines."

"Good. I will take care of my end of it immediately after lunch. Unless I am needed for something here, I will not come back but will go home and get ready for the trip."

"Fine. I don't think we will need you until you return to Moscow. When you reach Leningrad you are to get in touch with Comrade Shipshev at the Machine Trust. The following morning will be all right. It will give you a chance to see some of Leningrad before you go to work. It is one of our most beautiful cities. Have a good journey."

"Thank you," I said.

I walked on down the corridor, with Masinov following. When we were outside, I stopped and looked at him.

"As you know, I'm going to have lunch with Irina Simonova. After that I will stop and send a message to my company in Chicago. I imagine that will automatically be checked. Then I am going to the American Embassy, and after that directly to my apartment. I will stay there until I go out for dinner. So it should be safe for you to take the afternoon off, if you like."

He smiled. "It's not that simple. I will call in for orders while you are having lunch. Either way, I'll see you at the plane in the morning."

I went to my car and put the camera and tape recorder on the front seat. Then I drove straight to the National Hotel, parked, and once more used my handkerchief on the two pieces of equipment and on the steering wheel. I did the same with the door handle when I got out and locked the car.

Irina was waiting for me in the lobby. It seemed to me that she looked a little paler than usual. "Thanks for coming, Peter," she said immediately. "Can we go right into the dining room instead of to the bar?"

"Of course," I said.

We were met at the entrance to the restaurant by a waiter, who suggested a table against the wall. Perhaps he was just being helpful, but I told him we'd rather have another table that was in a dark corner. He nodded and led us to it. I ordered vodka for both of us, and we waited until he had served the drinks.

"I think I need this," Irina said softly when he was gone. "I had a rather bad morning." She lifted the glass and took a big swallow.

"I thought something was wrong when you phoned," I said. "Finish that and I'll order two more. Then we can talk. It should be safe here." I motioned to the waiter and ordered two more drinks. We were ready for them when he brought them.

"What happened?" I asked.

"I was taken to a large office in the Kremlin. There was a very old man there. His hair was white and there were many lines in his face. He did not tell me his name. He asked many questions about you and made some terrible suggestions."

ELEVEN

Somehow I wasn't surprised. I had already decided that the old man was like an old dog: once he thought he'd found a scent, he wouldn't let go. I was certain he'd had my office gone through the night before, looking for fingerprints. Finding none would only whet his eagerness. I didn't underestimate him. No matter who he was, he was certainly important, and it would be only a matter of time before he would clamp down on me.

He was old enough to be patient, but not old enough to be careless. Sooner or later, when his efforts to get my prints continued to fail, he'd simply have me arrested and have my prints taken. And there was still the problem of the message I'd received saying that one of the four agents was a traitor. All of them knew that I was an agent and knew my code name. The only thing they didn't know was my real name.

"I've met him," I told Irina. "That's where I was taken last night."

"Who is he?"

"I don't know," I said truthfully. "What did he want from you?"

"First, he asked me a lot of questions about you. He wanted to know about your work and what else you were interested in. He asked why you had wanted to visit the military centers and the prisons, but I think he was more interested in the prisons. Then he got more personal."

"How?"

"It wasn't so much what he said, but the way he said it. He wanted to know if we were lovers—although that is not the way he expressed it. Then he said he knew that I was going to Leningrad with you and that he wanted me to do two things—to get a sample of your fingerprints and send them to the KGB. And he wanted me to spend a lot of time in bed with you and try to get you to talk about other things and to report everything you said. He warned me that as a Soviet citizen it was my duty to do what he asked."

"How are you supposed to give your reports?"

"There's a KGB office in Leningrad. I'm supposed to hand them in there."

"Did you tell him that I was looking for Hartwell and Sorge?"

"Of course not," she said indignantly.

"I was just asking, honey," I said. "In the meantime, it's perfectly all right to try to get me to talk in bed."

She laughed, but she still sounded nervous. "I'm a little frightened, Peter. It's the first time I've ever been asked to do anything like this. I don't like it. Do you think they will find out that I work for you?"

"They might not," I said.

I wasn't going to tell her that it was very possible they already knew. Of course, it was also possible that she was the traitor, although I didn't believe it. But I had been wrong once or twice before.

We had two more drinks and lunch, and talked about other things. It was probably safe to talk where we were sitting, but it wasn't a good idea to talk seriously too long. This was a cat-and-mouse game, something the Russians were good at, and I expected the white-haired man was an expert. At the moment, I felt that it was just possible I was the mouse.

After lunch I walked out of the hotel with Irina. She told me where I could send my cablegram. I drove her to her office first and then went to file the cable. Then I drove to the American Embassy. I parked and again wiped prints off the steering wheel and door, before going inside.

At the desk I explained that I had forgotten my passport, left it in my apartment. I displayed my visa and the identity papers the Russians had given me and mentioned the man I had seen at the Embassy a few days before when I had checked in. There was considerable activity and I was finally shown into an office. While I waited, I used my pen to survey the room. The light went on once, which meant there was some sort of microphone there. I stepped outside and waited.

I recognized him before he even looked at me. Then I stepped forward to meet him. "Hello," I said. "You probably don't remember me, but I'm Peter Miloff. We met a few days ago. I'm here as a consultant for the Automatic Machine Trust."

Recognition came into his eyes. "Oh, yes. I remember you. I was expecting to find you in that room. Come on in."

"No," I said. "There's a bug in there and what I have to say must not be overheard."

He looked startled. "Are you sure?"

"Yes. I'll take you in and show you if you like. It's in the wall outlet immediately on the right as you go in."

"You have a way of detecting a bug?"

"Yes."

"We'll try another office," he said grimly.

He led the way down the corridor and opened a door. He motioned me in without saying anything, and I took out the pen and went over the room carefully. The light didn't go on.

"Seems to be all right," I said.

He came in and closed the door. "What's this all about, Mr. Miloff? I have a feeling I won't like it, but I'd better hear it."

"First, do you have an Intelligence liaison man on your staff? If so, I suggest that he should be in on this."

He looked even more unhappy. He started to reach for the phone, then quickly withdrew his hand, got up, and left the room. He was soon back with a man in uniform.

"This," he said, "is Mr. Miloff, an American citizen who is here as a consultant for the Automatic Machine Trust. Mr. Miloff, this is Sergeant MacDonald, our military attaché.

"Hello, Sergeant," I said. "I'll try to make all of this brief because they will be suspicious if I'm here too long. You know me as Peter Miloff, employed by the Brotherhood Coin Vending Company of Chicago. I was cleared on this job by the State Department, as I'm sure you also know. Peter Miloff is not my real name. It is not necessary for you to be told what it is; in fact, you're probably better off not knowing. I am here on two assignments for the Central Intelligence Agency. My code name is Uncle Vanya. If it's possible, you can check this with General Sam Roberts in Washington."

"I know General Roberts," the Sergeant said. "Do you have a code name for him?"

"Uncle Bobby."

The Sergeant looked at the Embassy man. "He gave the right answer. And I think I recognize him. He's right. It's better if the Embassy doesn't know his real name."

The Embassy man sighed as though the weight of the world were on his shoulders. "All right, Mr. Miloff. What do you want?"

I smiled at him. "My first request is an easy one. The Automatic Machine Trust has just filed a formal request to purchase four vending machines. I promised them I would ask you to inform the State Department that this is being done at my request. That is supposedly the reason I am here."

"We'll take care of it at once," he said. "What else?"

"Do you have any means of developing some film quickly without the Russians knowing about it?"

They looked at each other. "As a matter of fact," the Sergeant said, "we have a small darkroom right here in the Embassy. What is it?"

I took the microfilm from my pocket and handed it to him. "There are only four or five pictures on the film, but I believe they are important and that speed is essential. I'll explain after you get this started."

The Sergeant left the room without a word. The Embassy man and I waited in silence. Sergeant MacDonald was back soon.

"I assume," I said, "that you know the name James Hartwell?"

They both nodded. "We've been trying to locate him for weeks."

"Do you know what he looks like?"

They nodded again.

"I think his picture is on that film. He's in the Uzbekistan Prison. Or at least he was yesterday. I think he may still be there."

"But we checked that prison for him only a few weeks ago," the Embassy man said.

"I have an idea about it," I said. "They probably had him stashed away somewhere out in the boondocks. But all the activity about him made them think that he might be important enough to use as bait. I think they moved him into some place you had already checked and sat back to see if an American agent would come to rescue him. They are already suspicious of me, but they're not certain, so they probably won't take him away just yet. If the pictures turn out to be of Hartwell, you may be able to move fast and force them to put him on trial."

"How fast?" the Sergeant asked.

"I can't be exact, but I know they're breathing down my neck. If they catch me or even find out who I am, they'll hide him in some hole again. The KGB has copies of my fingerprints from years ago, and they are trying hard to get some fresh prints from me. In case you're wondering, Sergeant, Washington gave me explicit orders not to try to rescue him. That's why I'm here."

He smiled. "I was wondering, sir. I seem to remember that one of your specialties was breaking in and out of prisons."

"You remember too much for your own good—or for mine, I'm not sure which. Now, I've got some fingerprints I want developed and I must know who they belong to. What can we do about that?"

"That's a little tougher," the Sergeant said. "We have no such facilities here, and it would be impossible to get it done inside Russia. I could use Paris. There's a man going with a diplomatic pouch this evening and he could take it—if the prints aren't on anything too large."

"A cigarette lighter." I removed it from my pocket, being careful to touch only the ends. "The prints are on the sides, so be sure they don't get messed up. I imagine the developed prints may have to be sent to Washington, but try the CIA man in Paris first. I want to know if they belong to a man named Richard Sorge."

The Sergeant whistled softly.

"Sorge?" the Embassy man said, frowning. "I remember that name. Wasn't he executed more than twenty years ago?"

"That was the report," I said, "but Washington believes that he may still be alive, and I'm inclined to agree. How fast do you think we can get an answer, Sergeant?"

"Well, if it can be checked out in Paris, we should have an answer in twenty-four hours. If it has to be sent to Washington, it'll take several days."

"Too long," I said. "Who will you contact at the CIA in Paris?"

"I'm not sure. I thought perhaps Morrison, who I know slightly."

"Do you know Henri Flambeau?"

"No. I've seen his name in reports, but that's all."

"Well, get it to him and tell him that Milo needs it yesterday. Let me know the very minute you get an answer. I'll be at the Lenin Hotel in Leningrad. If the prints aren't those of Sorge, tell them to check against other old-time agents of the Soviet Union, but if that's the case I don't have to be told the answer. I only want to know if I've found Sorge."

"Why the need for so much speed?" the Sergeant asked. "What can you do about it if they are Sorge's?"

"I can get the hell out of the country. Whoever he is, he's already caught the scent and he's hot on my trail. And it might be shortened for him. There are four double agents here who know I'm an agent, although they don't know my real name. One of them is a leak. I don't know which one."

There was a knock on the door. It opened and an excited-looking young man stood there, waving a piece of microfilm in his hand. "Sergeant," he said, "do you know who this is?"

"We have a pretty good idea, but suppose you tell us?"

"Hartwell. I used a magnifying glass to examine the pictures. It's Hartwell, all right." Then, for the first time, he saw me. He stopped suddenly and his face paled.

"It's all right," I said. "I brought the film."

"Okay, Ross," the Sergeant said. "You can go back, but don't let that film out of your sight."

He left as I turned to the Embassy man. "May I suggest that you put some sort of twenty-four-hour-a-day watch on the prison? If it's possible, I'd like you to give me forty-eight hours before you move in to demand him. If you can't, then go ahead. I may get caught anyway, and he's one of the reasons I'm here, so don't let them stow him away again."

"We can use the photographs?"

"Yes, either way. Now I'd like one more thing. Some money."

"Dollars or rubles?"

"I'd prefer dollars, at least three thousand dollars. You'll be reimbursed through the usual channels."

"I think we can manage that much. I'll be right back." He left the room.

Sergeant MacDonald looked at me. "If we get an answer on the prints, how do you want us to get the message to you?"

"Let's use the simplest method instead of making like secret agents. Call me at my hotel and tell me that my message to the State Department was sent and is being considered favorably or unfavorably or they haven't answered yet. The clue will be in the word 'sent,' if the prints are those of Sorge. If they are not his, then tell me that you were slightly delayed in getting the message off, but it was sent and the rest the same."

"Sounds good enough. What do you do if they aren't Sorge's?"

I smiled. "Stick around as long as I can and do some more work. Only I'm getting tired of wiping my prints off of everything around me. ... Incidentally, there's a bug in the office where I was supposed to wait just now. It's behind the electric outlet just to the right as you enter."

"Thanks," he said. "I'll take care of it."

The door opened and the Embassy man came back in. He was carrying a slip of paper and a stack of bills. "I almost had to pick the Ambassador's pocket to make it, but here's the three thousand. It does bring up a problem."

"What?"

"You have to sign a release for it. Do you think they'll accept the name you're using?"

"Probably," I said, "but a lot of career men may faint before that happens. I'll tell you what I'll do. I'll sign my real name if you'll lock this in the safe and keep it there until I get out of the country."

"I think that will be all right," he said.

He handed me the paper and I signed it. I was amused to notice that he folded it up without looking at the signature.

"I'm leaving for Leningrad in the morning," I said. "I don't know how long I'll be there, but I have a feeling that I'll be trying to get away within two or three days. Thank you for everything."

"Thank you," the Sergeant said. "And good luck."

I left and went down to the car. Since there was no sign of Masinov, I figured he may have decided to take the rest of the day off. I drove straight back to my apartment and once more cleaned off the steering wheel and the door handle of the car. I carried the camera and tape recorder up to the apartment, where I went over everything carefully. I found traces of powder on a couple of glasses in the kitchen. Someone had been there. They'd been very careful but not quite careful enough.

I made myself a drink and stretched out on the couch and turned the radio on. I wasn't really tasting the cigarette I lit because I was tense—the way I always get when I know I'm coming down to the wire. I thought I could trust Irina, but I knew that from now on there were going to be a hundred eyes on me.

At least I knew I had completed half of the assignment. I had located James Hartwell. Personally, I still thought they should have told me to get him out if I could, but I was also glad I didn't have to do it. I might have enough trouble just getting myself out.

I picked up the phone and called Voukelitch. I told him I was sorry that I couldn't reach him earlier and that I was leaving Moscow the next morning. I added that I would be returning to the city and that perhaps it could be arranged for him to do some more articles then. I hung up, finished my drink, and took a nap.

When I awakened it was about time for me to hear from Marya. I shaved and showered and got dressed. While I was getting clothes out of the dresser, I checked on my gun. It hadn't been disturbed, so I was pretty certain that meant its hiding place hadn't been discovered. I was just coming out of the bedroom when there was a knock on the door.

It was Marya. I could see that she was upset again, but I insisted that she have a drink before we went to dinner. I fixed two drinks and she relaxed somewhat. When she had finished her drink, I took the glasses into the kitchen and washed them, wiping off the bottle I had used. As we left the apartment, I used my handkerchief on the door again.

"Peter," she said when we were out on the street, "I have to talk to you where they won't hear. Can we go into the park?"

"I don't think it's smart," I said. "Late at night it's romantic;

just before dinner it's suspicious. I think we can talk in the car. I'll check it again before we start."

We got into the car and I used my pen. There was no light.

"We can talk as we drive," I said, "but first you must tell me where we are going. I hope it's a good restaurant. I'll have to use a rear exit. Sometime during our cocktail hour I'm going to slip out for a half hour or so. I don't think we're being followed, but I want to play safe. It also has to be a fairly large restaurant so that my absence won't be too noticeable."

She thought for a minute as I started the car. "I think maybe the Aragvy. But it's expensive."

"Don't worry about that, honey."

"Keep straight ahead. I'll tell you when to turn. Do you know what happened to me today, Peter?"

"I can guess," I said. "Someone came and took you to the Kremlin, to an office where an old man sat and waited to talk to you. He was probably in a bad humor because he likes to work at night. He had white hair and a wrinkled face."

"How did you know?"

"I've been there. I can even tell you what he wanted. He asked you a lot of questions about me. Then he suggested that you go to bed with me tonight and try to get me to talk. And he also told you to try to get my fingerprints on something and give that to him."

"How could you know all of that, Peter?"

"Just talented," I said. "What else happened, Marya?"

"It was the way you described it. Only after he stopped asking about you, he turned on me. He knew everything about me, Peter."

"Everything? You mean he knew that you worked for the Americans?"

"He didn't mention that. But he knew I was an agent for my country and for Russia. He said I was a prostitute, but I could use my talent to get valuable information, only I had to be smart. I—I never felt so terrible in my life, Peter. He made me feel as if he'd stripped off all my clothes and was looking at me, but not with the eyes of a man. Do you know what I mean?"

"I know what you mean, honey. What else did he say?"

"That's all—except that he told me that I'd better get what he wanted from you. He said he could have me put in prison because I was an agent for my country, or that he could have me put in prison as a common prostitute. But the worst thing was the way he talked and looked at me ..." She looked up. "Turn right at the next street."

"I know how you feel, Marya," I said, "but try not to let it throw you too much. I know it's not easy, but right now there's nothing else to do but retreat—and that might be even more unpleasant. He's already asked someone else to do the same thing, and she's failed, so if you fail it won't be so bad. I'm going to Leningrad tomorrow morning, but I'll be back soon and we'll work out something for you. Just don't be too frightened. He's an old man still trying to live in the past."

"Where will you be in Leningrad?" she asked as though just knowing that would make a link between us.

"The Lenin Hotel."

"All right," she said. She sounded calmer. "Turn left at the next street and we'll be at the restaurant."

I did as she told me and parked. We went inside and found a table in the rear and in a corner. There were several people in the restaurant already, which was good. I ordered vodka for both of us, although I had to admit I was getting a little tired of vodka.

People continued to come in as we drank, but I didn't see anyone who looked like a tail. They were all couples or parties of four or six persons. We ordered two more drinks. Halfway through mine, I turned to Marya.

"I'm going now," I said. "I'll get back as quickly as I can. I don't think that anyone will notice, but if someone should ask about me, just tell them that I wasn't feeling well and stepped outside for a bit of fresh air. If you want, order another drink and tell the waiter I'll be right back to finish mine."

"All right, Peter," she said.

I got up and strolled toward the back. I spotted the restrooms and then, just beyond them, a door. No one else was around, so I just marched through the door. I found myself in a dark area. Just beyond it was another restaurant. I noticed there was a taxi parked in front of it. I sprinted and got there before anyone else. I told the driver where I wanted to go.

When we arrived, I tipped the driver heavily and told him there would be that much more for him if he waited. He said he would. I walked down to the restaurant, where Nuritdin was standing. I nodded to him and kept walking. He caught up with me.

"I have what you wanted," he said. "We will turn at the next corner and then I will deliver it to you."

We turned as he suggested and he finally stopped, near

enough to a streetlight so I could see what I was getting and he could count the money. He handed me my old passport and then the new one. It was a good job. I counted out the balance of the payment in dollars and gave it to him.

On the way back I stopped in at the restaurant. Zoubov was there. This time I sat at a table and ordered a drink. After it was served, I indicated to Zoubov that he should join me. He walked over, a drink in his hand.

"I was going to ignore you," he said, "but then I figured you might have something important to say. You're big enough to take care of yourself."

"What's that supposed to mean?"

"There's fuzz in the place tonight. He's been tailing me, but I'm sure he saw you meet Nuritdin outside. Now you're talking to me, so he'll probably follow you. Guy at the corner table."

"Thanks for the tip," I said. "I'll take care of it. I just wanted to tell you that I'm going to Leningrad tomorrow. I'm supposed to return here sometime soon, but I'm not sure that I will. I may decide to take a powder. I'll get your message to Benotti. You should be getting a letter from your family before long."

"How come the powder?"

"There's some heat on me from some big-shot fuzz."

"Okay," he said. "I'll wait to hear from my family." He stood up and walked back to his table.

I finished my drink, put money on the table, and stood up. Without seeming to do so, I was watching the other people. I saw one man hurrying to pay his bill. That was the man

Zoubov had mentioned. I walked out through the front door and stopped, looked up and down the street, and managed to see that the man had begun to follow me but had stopped and was pretending to count his change.

So I was being followed.

TWELVE

Lighting a cigarette, I glanced up and down. Finally I saw what I was looking for. There were four youths coming down the street. They were all big boys and they were wearing clothes that might have been bought in America. They were *stilyagi,* Moscow's equivalent of hippies. I had remembered that they hung around this section, and had been hoping I would spot them. I walked in their direction, and stopped in front of them.

"Zdravstvuyte," I greeted them. "I would like to ask a favor of you."

They stared at me, but there was no fear in their eyes. "What sort of favor?" one of them asked.

"There is a man who is following me. You should be able to see him."

They looked past me. "I see a man," the same one said. "He is standing on the street, looking around as if he were lost."

"That's the one," I said. "I do not want to be followed. I will give you fifty dollars—American dollars—if you will see that he is delayed long enough so that he cannot follow me."

"Where did you get dollars?" one of them asked.

"I have them," I said. I reached into my pocket. I knew that the roll I'd gotten from the Embassy had fifty-dollar bills on the outside, so I separated one and brought it out.

"I have the dollars," I said.

They hesitated, staring at me. I was sure that they were thinking that they might get the money and more by just knocking me out.

"We could just take the fifty dollars," one said.

"You could try," I said gently.

"How do we know that you're not from the police?" another one asked.

"Who would trust a policeman with fifty dollars?" I asked.

They laughed. "How do we know it's good?"

"Ask Nuritdin."

"You know Nuritdin?"

"Yes. I just left him."

"All right," one of them said. "Give us the money and we will delay your companion."

I handed him the fifty dollars and walked past them without looking back. I hadn't walked far before I heard the sound of voices and then of blows behind me. I kept on walking until I reached the taxi, got in, and told the driver to take me back to the Aragvy. As we drove away, I looked through the rear window. There was nobody in sight except the figure of a man lying on the street.

I had been gone only twenty-five minutes when I slipped back into my chair beside Marya. "Everything all right?" I asked her.

"Yes. No one asked any questions. I did order another drink."

"Good." I finished what was left of mine and beckoned to the waiter. "Two more."

We had them and then ordered dinner. I had shashlik and she had chicken tabaka. Both were good. We had some pastry later and then tea and brandy. They didn't have any coffee. We drove back to the apartment. Once more I cleaned off the fingerprints before leaving the car.

"Peter," she said as we walked down the street, "you are nervous tonight."

"Yes. I'm nervous. But it'll be all right, honey."

"Are you afraid, Peter?"

"No more than usual," I said honestly. "I always get nervous as things progress. It only makes me work better."

"I am frightened," she said simply. "I need your strength."

"We'll work our way through it," I told her. "I just have to do a few things. One of them is to find Sasha. But I don't know where to start looking."

"I'll try," she said. "Honestly, I will."

I patted her on the shoulder and we went into the building. As soon as we were in my apartment, I turned on the radio, putting the volume fairly high.

Marya was still upset, and again she drank too much and too fast. Within a couple of hours she had passed out again. I sighed and picked her up and put her to bed. She'd have to explain the lack of silence the next day, but I'd talk to her about it in the morning. I had another drink and went to bed myself.

I awakened in plenty of time the next morning. I showered and checked to see if I needed a shave. I didn't. I got dressed and then began to pack my clothes. When I'd finished that, I went into the kitchen and put the coffee on. Then I made two Bloody Marys and put out the smoked fish and the rolls, carried the drinks into the bedroom, put them down, and stroked her face. She came back to consciousness the same way she had before: first the peering through slit eyes, her face full of fear, then finally spotting me and changing. I thought to myself that she was very close to cracking up—and therefore she was potentially dangerous.

I put my fingers to my lips and then indicated with hand signals that I wanted her to speak to me as if she'd brought the drinks for me. She blinked at me for a moment, but she was smart and caught on right away.

"Peter," she said. "I have some medicine for you." I could tell by her expression that she didn't know what was going on, but she played along with it.

"Thanks, honey," I said. I deliberately slurred my speech so it would sound as if I was just waking up. I took a drink. "Just what the doctor ordered. I'm sorry about last night, honey."

"That's all right, Peter," she said. She still didn't know what we were really talking about. She didn't have to as long as she gave the right answers.

"I guess I've been working very hard and I just had too much to drink. It's late. I've got to make that plane. Be a good girl and get something out for breakfast. I'll take a shower and then we can have breakfast."

I pointed to her and motioned toward the shower. She nodded, gulped some more of her drink, and slipped out of bed. As she vanished into the bathroom, I went back to the kitchen. I made noises with the plates and knives and forks until she finally appeared.

"Well," I said, "I think I feel a little better. Thanks, honey."

We finished breakfast and she got dressed. I knew she had to get changed, so I said good-bye to her and picked up my luggage. We both walked out of the apartment. I waited until we were in the corridor and the apartment door was closed.

"Marya," I said, "you can explain not having any information by telling them that I got drunk and passed out last night. That was the reason for the conversation this morning. I'll see you when I get back." I kissed her and went downstairs.

I put the luggage in the car and went back to the apartment. Once more I made certain about the fingerprints, then carried the camera and tape recorder down to the car. I had already tucked the gun under my belt on my left side, far enough back so that it wouldn't show. I had decided I might need it anytime from now on.

I stopped once to ask a policeman how to get to the airport, and then drove straight there. I cleaned off the key and left it in the ignition switch. I wiped the steering wheel—for the last time, I hoped—and other spots where I might have left prints, hung the camera around my neck, tucked the tape recorder under my arm, and picked up my luggage. I kicked the door shut and went into the terminal.

As soon as I arrived, somebody took the luggage from me to put on the plane—and probably to check for prints. Somebody else came up and asked me for the keys to the car and the apartment. I told him the car key was in the ignition and handed him the apartment key. He disappeared.

Masinov was already there. Irina arrived a few minutes

later. We were then told to board the plane. We were the only passengers, and it took off as soon as we were in our seats.

It was a relatively short flight to Leningrad, and I slept most of the way. We were met at the airport by a car and driven to the hotel. It seemed all three of us were staying at the same place. I was amused to notice that Irina had the room next to mine and there was a connecting door. Masinov was on the floor below us.

I checked my room. There were two bugs in it. That was about par for the course, since it was a large room. There was a small alcove at one end of the room. There were no cooking facilities, but a small refrigerator was there. It looked as if it had just been moved in. There was also a plentiful supply of liquor and glasses. I smiled to myself. They wanted to be sure that I had plenty of opportunities to loosen my tongue.

I unpacked a few things and put them away, then made myself a drink. By the time I'd finished it, I decided it was a good idea to get on the job. I knocked on the connecting door.

"Yes?" Irina asked.

"Are you ready?" I called. "I want to get started."

"I'll meet you in the lobby," she answered.

I went downstairs and asked the clerk to tell Mr. Masinov that I was there. Then I sat down and lit a cigarette. Irina showed up first and Masinov was there immediately afterward. We went outside and there was the same car and driver that had brought us from the airport. We were driven to the Machine Trust Building. It was smaller than the one in Moscow; so was my office. I left Irina and Masinov in it while I went to see Shipshev.

He turned out to be quite different from Ivanov. He was a little man with a harassed expression, who neither smiled nor offered to shake hands.

"We understand," he said, "that you've done very good work in Moscow and are looking forward to what you can suggest for us. Would you mind telling me how you plan to approach this?"

"Much the same way as I did in Moscow. I'll visit large marketplaces, factories, business offices, military establishments, and any large prisons. I will photograph logical spaces for the installation of machines and will dictate reports on what sort of machines should be installed. I will also have discussions with you and will include any other spots you suggest."

"That sounds all right," he said. "I was told that those were the places that would be considered. I have had a list of such places made up for you." He handed me a sheet of paper. "When do you plan to start?"

"Today. May I ask if you have arranged for me to have the use of a car while I'm here?"

"I have had no instructions about that, but I have arranged for you to have the use of the car and driver which brought you here."

"I prefer a car that I can drive myself. Not only because of the work, but in my spare time I'd like to get around and see some of the sights of Leningrad."

"I have no instructions about that," he repeated. He looked as if he were about to cry.

"All right," I said. "I'll see you later."

I went back to my office. "Comrade Masinov," I said, "am I permitted to telephone Moscow?"

"Did you forget something?" he countered.

"No, but somebody did. I want to phone Nikolai Ivanov."

"I imagine you can," he said. "Get the operator and tell her who you want."

I picked up the phone and told the operator how to reach Ivanov. It took a few minutes, but then he came on the phone.

"Comrade Miloff," he exclaimed, "it is a surprise to hear from you. Is everything all right?"

"Not quite," I said. "I have a complaint. I expected to be treated the same way here that I was in Moscow. But I discover it is impossible for me to get a car to use, although I have been assigned a large car and chauffeur. I am not an American capitalist and I'm not accustomed to such things. Besides, I like to be able to get around the city when I'm not working. If you remember, I like my social life."

"I don't understand it," he said, "and I am sorry that it has happened. I will phone Comrade Shipshev at once, and we will get it straightened out. Is that all, Comrade Miloff?"

"I think so. I'll see you soon—when I get back to Moscow."

"I will look forward to it," he said. "When everything is well advanced, we must have dinner together."

I hung up and looked at them. There was a little smile on Irina's face and Masinov was grinning openly.

"I have to say one thing for you," he said. "You have nerve."

"Why not?" I said. "Your government is paying me a lot of money to do a job for them. How well I work—or how well anyone works—depends on how I'm treated. I did the preliminary work in Moscow in about one-tenth the time they expected me to take. I want to be treated the same way here or any other place I go. It saves the government money. Any fool can figure that out. Let's go."

The three of us left the office and walked down the hallway. I stopped at Shipshev's office, looking at Masinov.

"You're the official authority around here," I said. "See if the director has changed his mind—or should I commit suicide?"

Masinov laughed and knocked on the door, then opened it. Shipshev was sitting at his desk, and he still looked as if he were about to cry.

"Ah," he said uncertainly, "there will be a car for you downstairs in a matter of minutes, Miloff. You may use it during your stay in Leningrad."

"Thank you," I said. "What about a car for Comrade Masinov?"

That stopped him. "I—I assumed he would ride in the car with you."

"You made a mistake," I said gravely. "Comrade Simonova will ride with me. Comrade Masinov is my security agent. He is supposed to protect me from the wild Russians. He can hardly do that while riding in the same car. He needs a separate car so that he can spot any trouble before it starts. Why don't you give him the big car and the chauffeur?"

His face lit up. "An excellent idea."

The phone rang. He picked it up, listened for a minute, and replaced the receiver. He looked up at me, his face more or less tranquil. "The car is downstairs for you. It is a Pobeda, which I trust is satisfactory."

"That is fine. I thank you."

"It is nothing," he said.

We marched out and went downstairs. When we left the front entrance, the big car with its chauffeur was directly ahead of us, and there was a Pobeda parked in front of it. A man stood beside the Pobeda. Masinov stopped and looked at me with interest.

"You are suddenly different, Comrade Miloff," he said. "You sound like a commissar."

"In a way, I am," I told him. "No Peter Miloff, no automatic machines. It is an old capitalist philosophy."

"And an old criminal philosophy?"

"Could be," I said with a smile. "But let's go to work. That is also an old capitalist philosophy."

Irina and I went to the Pobeda. I identified myself to the man who had brought the car and he gave me the keys. Irina and I got in the car. While I fiddled around getting it started, I made a quick check with my pen. There was no sign of any listening device. I hadn't expected one. They hadn't really had enough time. I started the motor and drove off.

I stopped the first time I saw a policeman and asked directions to the factory that was on top of the list. We pulled away as he had directed.

"Peter," Irina said, "there's something wrong, isn't there?"

"There are a lot of things wrong, honey," I said. I took a deep breath and plunged ahead. "Irina, I have made contact with four American agents in Moscow. Two of them are double agents, one is a triple agent, and the fourth one is you. One of you four is not really working for us. I don't know which one."

"Peter, that's terrible!" she said. She giggled. "I guess that's the wrong thing to have said. I should have said, 'Not poor little me.' "

"I don't think so," I said. "Tell me one thing, Irina. Do you still want to go to America?"

"Of course. As soon as I can."

"How would you like to go in the next few days?"

She looked startled. "What do you mean? How could I do that?"

"You might be able to go with me—if I make it. But I also think it will be dangerous for you to stay here. I think it's very possible that someone already knows about you. If I do manage to get out, it will then be worse for you here. As I see it, you have two choices, honey. You can stick with me and we either get out or we don't, or you can go tell someone all about me and hope that they will forgive you for past indiscretions."

"Peter," she exclaimed, "I would never do that!"

"Well, it's one of your choices. That white-haired man you saw is hot on my trail. That's why he wants my fingerprints. So far I've outsmarted him on that score, but sooner or later I have to overlook something. Once he gets my fingerprints, it's all over."

"Why don't you leave at once, then?"

"I'm waiting to find out if I completed my two assignments. If I haven't, then I can't leave."

"Even if you know that you may be arrested any minute?"

"Even then. I can't stand an untidy house."

"But—but how can you get out?"

"From here? By land or sea."

"What about Masinov?"

"There are several things about Masinov," I said. I'd gone this far with her, so I might as well go a little further. "He's one of the four agents I mentioned, which means that he also may be the leak. However, I think I can avoid him long enough to get away."

She was silent for a minute. "And what will happen to me if I go with you, Peter?"

"As soon as we get out of the Soviet Union, you will go with me to the American Embassy and ask for political asylum. I will speak to someone in Washington, which will hurry things up. You already have a record of working for us and must even have some money due you. There will be a period of questioning, and then you will have the chance of staying in America and eventually becoming a citizen."

"But getting out may be dangerous, no?"

"It may. Once I'm gone, it will also be dangerous."

She was silent for a moment as I drove. Then she put her hand lightly on mine. "I will go with you, Peter, and take whatever happens."

THIRTEEN

She left her hand there while we drove two or three blocks. I glanced at her. Her face was very pale, but she didn't seem to be coming apart at the seams. I had an idea that she was going to be all right.

"Now," I said, "forget about it for the moment. We'll just do our work and forget everything else until it's time."

She nodded. "All right, Peter."

We spent the rest of the day in factories, finishing the list before we returned to the office. I turned over the film I had exposed to Shipshev, and then Irina and I drove back to the hotel, followed by Masinov.

"Irina," I said, "when we reach the hotel, we'll have a couple of drinks in my room. Then I'm going to tell you that I want to take a nap before we go out for dinner, and send you back to your room. I'm going to slip out of the hotel for a short time. You can stay in your room or go downstairs or do whatever you want to do. I'll be back as quickly as I can, but I'll probably be gone one or two hours at least."

"I understand," she said quietly. Now that her decision was made, she seemed calm. She was going to be all right.

We went up to my room and I fixed two drinks. While we had them, I talked to her about the work for that afternoon. She fell in with it and asked questions that would seem to be logical for her series of articles. Finally we finished our drinks.

"Irina," I said, "I'm a little tired. I think I'll take a nap before we go to dinner."

"All right, Peter. I'll be in my room whenever you're ready."

She crossed the room and used the connecting door. I took the glasses into the bathroom and washed them. Then I sat down on the bed and took off my shoes, dropping them to the floor. I flopped on the bed and sighed heavily. I was glad to know that the bed didn't make a lot of noise.

After several minutes I sat up carefully and put my shoes on. Then I walked silently across the room and opened the door. I closed it behind me, but didn't try to lock it. That might make just enough noise to be picked up by the microphone.

I went down the stairs instead of taking the elevator. There was a mezzanine floor. I stopped there and took a good look at the lobby. Masinov was nowhere in sight, so I walked on down and out the front door. About three blocks up the street I stopped to light a cigarette. I couldn't spot anyone following me. I found a taxi and asked the driver to take me down to the waterfront. As he drove off, I checked again through the rear window. There didn't seem to be anyone behind us.

The taxi deposited me near the docks. I checked to make sure that I could get another taxi there, then paid the driver. I walked past dozens of boats and finally found a small bar. Inside, it was filled with men, most of them well along in years, their faces weather-beaten and rough. I found a place at the bar and ordered vodka, sipping it slowly and looking around. Most of the men were at the bar, drinking vodka and bragging about the fish they'd caught. There was one old man alone at the end of the bar. He was drinking a beer and paying no attention to the others. I finished my drink and moved down next to him.

I ordered another vodka and looked at the old man. "May I buy you a vodka?" I asked him.

He glanced at me curiously. "You are a stranger," he said.

"Yes. I just arrived from Moscow today."

"You are not a fisherman?"

"No. I work with machines."

"Ah," he said. "You may buy me a vodka—unless you are afraid of bad luck."

I nodded to the bartender, who was waiting, and he brought the old man a drink, which I paid for.

"We will drink to better luck," I said, lifting my glass. "My name is Peter Miloff."

"Pyotr Yegorov," he said, raising his glass.

We drank and I ordered two more. "Now," I said when they had been delivered, "what is this nonsense about bad luck?"

He shrugged. "It is a fact. This year the fish have not been biting for me and they have been biting for everyone else. There was a time when I would go light a candle, but those days were done with a long time ago. Now it is only bad luck."

"If it were not for bad luck, how much would you have made this year?"

"Perhaps two thousand rubles. But what's the difference?"

"Who knows? What kind of boat do you have?"

"A good one. Motor-driven. It will carry three or four persons."

"How would you like to have either three thousand rubles or three thousand dollars in American money?"

He glanced at me out of the corners of his eyes. "I need another drink while I think about that."

I motioned to the bartender, who served us again. I paid and the bartender went away.

"So," the old man said softly, "you are one of those who would like to take a night trip. Where?"

"Helsinki."

"It is not a long trip. When would I get this money?"

"Five hundred now and the rest when we're off the shore of Helsinki."

"How do I know that you have such wealth?"

I reached into my pocket and pulled out money. I held it below the level of the bar. "Look."

He glanced down and his eyes got bigger. "When?"

"I'm not sure, but probably tomorrow night or the night after."

"At what time?"

"That would be up to you. Whatever you think is the best time."

"After midnight," he said thoughtfully, and I knew he was hooked. "It is a short journey, but there will be fewer patrols at that time. Everyone knows of my bad luck, so they will only laugh if they find me out fishing at night. How many persons?"

"Myself and one other."

"All right," he said. "If I were younger I might even go myself. I will take dollars. I can make a small profit on the black market."

"I know," I said. I pulled the money from my pocket again and counted out five hundred dollars and passed it to him. He put it in his pocket.

"If we do not go tomorrow night, I will come here at about this time to let you know. If I am not here early, then I will come at about midnight. I will merely come into the bar and have one drink, then leave, and wait for you to lead the way to your boat."

He nodded. "How do you know that I will not take what you've already given me and not show up again?"

"I don't," I said with a smile. "But there is much more waiting for you, and I have always believed that all fishermen are honest. Of course, if I am wrong, there is always this." I parted my coat enough so he could get a glimpse of the gun.

"I can see that you are a man of experience," he said. "I will be here."

I finished my drink and left the bar. After I'd found a taxi, I had the driver take me to within two blocks of the hotel. I walked down the street, keeping a sharp watch on the other pedestrians. When I reached the hotel, I discovered there was a side entrance leading directly into the bar. I glanced inside. There were only four customers, and Masinov was not one of them. I went in and ordered a drink. Halfway through it, I went to the phone and called Irina's room.

"Peter," I said when she answered. "I woke up and came down to the bar. Why don't you join me and then we'll see about having dinner?"

"I'll be right down," she said.

She was there within five minutes. I ordered her a drink. She took a quick gulp when it arrived, then grabbed my arm and hugged it to her.

"I am glad to see you," she said.

"I wasn't gone that long," I told her.

"Long enough to make me worry," she said.

"I didn't stay any longer than I had to. I think I have everything arranged for us. Now all we have to do is wait."

"That is the hardest part, Peter."

We had a couple of drinks and then decided to try our luck in the hotel restaurant. She was not very familiar with Leningrad, and neither of us felt like exploring.

The food was good and we took our time over it. Then we went upstairs to my room. I had coached her during dinner, and we went through a period of her trying to get information out of me for the benefit of the microphones. Then we went to bed.

The next morning we had breakfast in the hotel and then drove to the office, followed by Masinov in his limousine.

"We're only going to work a half day," I told Irina on the way. "Then I'm going back to the hotel to dictate reports."

"Why?"

"I'm hoping I will get a phone call, and I don't want to miss it."

We checked into the office and then immediately left to cover a number of business offices. At noon, we returned to the Machine Trust Building so I could deliver the film, and then went back to the hotel. Irina came into my room with me. I made us a couple of drinks and then started dictating my report. When she had finished her drink, I sent her out to get us sandwiches and tea. We were both getting more tense.

I had been dictating for a couple of hours when the phone rang. I picked up the receiver and said hello.

"Mr. Miloff," a voice said in English, "this is MacDonald at the American Embassy in Moscow. I thought I should let you know that your recommendation concerning purchases of machinery was sent to the State Department and is being considered favorably."

"Thank you," I said gravely. "I hope they will expedite the shipment."

"I'm sure they will."

"Well, thanks again for phoning me. I'll probably stop in when I get back to Moscow."

I hung up and gave Irina a big smile to indicate the news was good. Then I went back to my dictating. It was difficult but necessary.

I had just finished, after another two hours, when the phone rang again. I wasn't expecting that one. I picked up the receiver and answered.

"Peter?" a feminine voice asked.

"Yes."

"This is Marya."

"Where are you?" I asked.

"In Leningrad. I'm at the Gorky Hotel. Room two-twenty. I bring regards from your close friend Sasha. I would like to see you."

"All right, Marya," I said.

I replaced the receiver and looked at Irina. I could see the strain on her face. "It was someone I know from Moscow. I'll give her a call later. In the meantime, I've just finished. Let's go downstairs and have a proper drink in the bar."

I put on my jacket and we went down. We ordered a couple of drinks and waited until the bartender had moved away.

"Who called?" she asked then.

"Another agent. She's here and seemed to indicate that she knows something about Sasha. She's at the Gorky Hotel. Do you know where that is?"

She shook her head. "I'll look it up," she said, sliding from the stool.

She was back soon. "It's on the street that parallels the docks on the Baltic Sea. Do you want to know how to find it?"

"I know where it is," I said. I ordered two more drinks and paid for them, then I took one sip from mine. "I'm going to get a taxi and go down there. I'll get back as quickly as I can. If I'm gone too long, go up to your room and wait for me—but only if you're beginning to feel conspicuous. I'll try to make it fast."

"Good luck, Peter," she whispered.

I went outside and found a taxi. I told him where I wanted to go without naming the hotel, and had him let me out in front of the dock. I could see the hotel down the street. I waited until he was gone, then walked swiftly to the hotel and looked inside. The clerk was not in sight. I stepped in and ducked up the stairway. I found room two-twenty without any trouble. I knocked gently.

There was no answer. Using my handkerchief, I tried the door. It opened easily. I stepped inside and closed the door.

She was there, lying in the middle of the floor. The front of her dress was covered with blood. It wasn't completely dry, but she was dead.

I felt awful about it, but there was nothing to be accomplished by just standing there. She'd been shot. Someone should be there to investigate the shot. If they weren't, maybe someone was around to see who would show up.

I used the handkerchief to let myself out and went downstairs. The clerk still wasn't at the desk and there was nobody else in the lobby. I hurried out to the street and walked a couple of blocks before I stopped to think. I finally crossed the street and walked along the shoreline. I passed the bar I'd been at the night before and continued walking. There was nothing but a string of empty, bobbing boats.

Poor Marya. She was frightened and ashamed of herself, but she had made a desperate effort to help me. She must have known that it was dangerous for her to come to Leningrad and to phone me. But she had done it. She'd had information about Sasha. That must be the leak. Sasha was the one person who might know the identity of all the other agents, but they wouldn't know him. I started putting the pieces together.

"What's wrong, Miloff?" the voice asked from behind me. "Mourning your little girlfriend?"

I turned around. It was Masinov. "Hello, Sasha," I said quietly.

He laughed. "You are smart," he said, "but too late. I wondered what would make you break. So it was little Marya."

"Did you have to kill her?" I asked dully.

"Why not? She was nothing but a whore. And it brought you out into the open."

"If you're Sasha," I said, "then you already knew I was an agent. Why didn't you just tell your white-haired friend and get it over with?"

"Why should I help him?" he asked with contempt. "He is an old man. I am young. I will help myself. I will deliver what he cannot. Then they will know that the young can do what the old fail in."

"What is that?" I asked.

"You," he said with a smile.

"Me?" I asked. "You think I'm something special?"

"I know you are."

"What?"

"I do not know exactly, but I know you are important. If you were not, the old man wouldn't be so anxious to get your fingerprints and you would not be so anxious to keep him from getting them. But there is one easy way to get them."

"What is that, Sasha?" I asked softly. I had already unbuttoned my jacket and was ready. I could also count on the same thing he was counting on: the waves were making a lot of noise and there was no one near us.

He laughed again. "It will be easy to take your fingerprints once you are dead, Comrade Miloff. You Americans are so stupid. You have paid me a lot of money for doing nothing. So I will stop getting money from you, but I will get something more valuable than your money could ever give me."

"You're wrong, Grigory."

"What do you mean?"

"What you will get is very cheap," I said. I pulled out the gun and shot him in the belly.

His face was convulsed with surprise and pain. His hands grabbed at his stomach and the blood spurted between his fingers. He coughed once and tried to reach for his gun. In the middle of reaching, he suddenly stumbled and fell on the sand. I walked over and made certain that he was finished. Without bothering about fingerprints, I tossed my gun over near the water.

I went back to his body and pulled out his gun. I looked at it. One shot had been fired. I turned and fired two fast shots into the water. Then I wiped off the gun and placed it in his hand, making sure that his prints were fixed on it. I walked back to the edge, where my gun was lying, dipped my Peter Miloff passport in the water, and tossed it on the sand.

I looked around. There was still no one in sight. I took off my jacket, checked the pockets, then ripped it in several places. I tossed it to the edge of the water. I kicked up the sand as though there had been a struggle. Then I walked away without looking back.

There was a taxi on the street about three blocks away. I got in and told the driver to take me to the Lenin Hotel. When I got there, I went directly to my room. I reached for a fresh jacket, and then, as an afterthought, I put on a sweater and then the jacket. I went back down to the bar.

"Is everything all right?" Irina asked as I sat down next to her.

"Everything is fine," I said.

I didn't feel that way; I felt old and tired. But there wasn't anything else to say. I finished the drink in front of me. "Let's go to dinner," I said, and looked at her. "Go to your room and put on something warmer."

She nodded and left. She was back in five minutes.

We went out and got into the Pobeda, driving around until we found a restaurant that was not too far from the sea. I also noticed that the place had a back entrance.

I think the dinner was good, but I didn't pay too much attention. When we'd finished, we went out and got into the car again. I drove around, staying near the waterfront, until I saw a movie house. I parked and we went inside. Irina went along, saying nothing.

They were showing old Soviet movies and they were very good, but I'm afraid I wasn't watching carefully. I could feel that Irina was equally tense. I kept my eye on the time. Finally I nudged her.

"Let's go, honey," I said.

We walked out of the theater and found a taxi, which we took to within a block of my meeting place. We walked across the street. There was a dark space beside a building.

"Wait there," I told her. "I won't be long."

She went obediently into the shadows, and I walked down to the bar. The old man was there. I stopped at the near end of the bar and had a vodka. Then I bought a bottle and left. The old man came out soon after.

"We are going?" he asked.

"Yes," I said. "It must be tonight."

He nodded and led the way. As we walked past Irina, she

came out and fell into step with me. We walked another hundred yards and the old man stopped at a boat.

"Go aboard," he said. "I will cast off."

I helped Irina aboard and then I jumped on. The old man loosened the rope and tossed it onto the deck. He gave the boat a shove and scrambled on. When the boat had drifted out far enough, he went to the motor. "Go below," he said.

Irina and I ducked into the small cabin. A moment later the motor started and we could feel the boat moving away slowly. It seemed like a half hour had passed, but it was probably no more than five or ten minutes when the old man called out and said we could come up if we wanted to.

We went up on the deck and could see the lights of Leningrad some distance behind us. Those were the only lights we could see. I brought out the bottle of vodka and offered it to the old man. He took a healthy swig and handed it back. I gave it to Irina and she took a drink. Then I had one.

"I thought it might be rough," the old man said, "but it looks like it may be all right."

"Why did you expect it to be rough?" I asked.

"There was a KGB officer killed on the beach this afternoon. The story is that he must have had a fight with an enemy of the State and they killed each other, but the other man must've fallen in the water and was carried off by the tide. They found his gun, his coat, and his passport, but that was all. I thought the police would be out, but I haven't seen them."

"Maybe they think they have it solved," I said.

"Perhaps," he answered. "It will be cold as we get farther

out. You may want to go below where it will be warmer. You may even sleep if you like. I will wake you when we get there."

"Thanks," I said. I took Irina's hand and we went back to the small cabin. We had another drink from the bottle.

"Peter," she said, "the KGB man who was killed …"

"Was Masinov," I said flatly. "He killed Marya and was going to kill me. He was also Sasha—the leak. But he was ambitious, so he didn't leak too much. He was going to make himself a big man."

"You killed him?"

"Yes. Does that bother you?"

"I guess not. I think what was bothering me was that you could have been killed."

"That's the name of the game, honey," I said. "Let's try to get some rest while we can. We'll need our strength."

"All right, Peter."

"And you might as well start learning my real name. It's not Peter Miloff. It's Milo March."

"Milo March," she repeated. "I like that."

We had a couple of drinks out of the bottle, then went to sleep with her head on my shoulder.

We were awakened by the old man. I could feel that the boat was moving slowly on low throttle. I was instantly awake.

"Is there something wrong?" I asked.

"No," he said. "We are almost at the shore and daylight is coming fast. We must move in and land you quickly."

I went up on deck and looked around. Everything was in the gray half light of early morning, but I could see the city and off to the left a dock with boats bobbing at the length of their mooring lines.

"I will land you to the right of the dock," the old man said. "It is safer there. Now, comrade, there is a small difference between us."

"I hadn't forgotten," I told him. I pulled money from my pocket and counted out the $2,500. "We'll leave the vodka with you, too. It will comfort you on the long trip back."

"Not as much as this," he said, putting the money in his pocket, "but I thank you."

In a few minutes we stepped off the boat. We waved silently as the old man turned the boat and drifted away. We had to scramble up a slight slope, and then we were standing on a street in Helsinki.

FOURTEEN

The city was slowly coming to life as we walked along. Deliveries were being made, and here and there people were on their way to work. No one paid any attention to us. Irina reached over and took my hand.

We walked seven or eight blocks before I finally spotted a taxi. We were in luck. The driver spoke a little English and was willing to accept American money for his fare. I told him to take us to the American Embassy.

It didn't look like anyone was up yet, but I didn't want to wait around until the normal routine had started. I put my finger on the button beside the door and held it there for a time.

The door finally opened and a man stood blinking at us. He was dressed, but obviously not fully awake. He was probably a servant.

"I am an American citizen," I began before he could say anything. "I realize that it's very early, but this is an emergency. I must see someone as quickly as possible. Do you have an intelligence or military attaché here?"

"Yes, but no one is up yet. If you could come back later ..."

"We can't. Wake up the officer." I stepped inside, pulling Irina with me.

The man looked unhappy, but led the way into a large room. "I will see what I can do," he said, and disappeared.

We waited. Almost thirty minutes went by before someone appeared. He was an Army captain and he didn't look too pleased. "Now, what's the problem?" he asked impatiently.

"Sorry to bother you so early, Captain," I said. "I am Major Milo March. It is imperative that I talk at once with General Sam Roberts in Washington."

"Do you have any proof of your identity, Major?"

"Only my passport." I produced the forged document.

He looked at it, but didn't really examine it closely. "This is highly unusual," he said. "I suppose we can put in the call, and if General Roberts accepts it you may talk to him. Where do we reach him? The Pentagon?"

"No." I gave him the number, and I could tell by his reaction that he had at least heard of the number. He glanced at Irina.

"And the young lady?"

"She is a citizen of the Soviet Union who has done work for us for some time. She is requesting political asylum. General Roberts will also take care of that."

He walked over to a table and picked up a phone. Then he put in the call and waited. Finally he reacted to a voice on the other end.

"General Roberts?" he asked. He apparently got an affirmative. "This is Captain Marshall in the Helsinki embassy. There is a man here who claims that he is Major Milo March and insists that he must speak to you at once." He listened a minute, then said, "Yes, sir." He handed me the phone.

"Hello, General," I said.

"Milo, what the hell are you doing in Helsinki?"

"Talking to you, sir."

"Then why are you there?"

"Mission completed, and there was a certain amount of speed indicated. At the moment my only identification is a forged passport." Out of the corner of my eyes I could see the Captain wince. "Now, you have to get busy and get us out of here before all hell breaks loose. Do I make myself clear?"

"Us?" he asked suspiciously.

"Yes. Do you recall the name of Irina Simonova?"

He was silent for a few seconds. "Yes."

"She's with me and is making an official request for political asylum."

"Just a minute, Milo." I could hear him rustling some papers. Then he came back on. "There's a military jet bomber in Helsinki at the moment, scheduled to leave soon. I'll see that you get on it. Now, let me talk to the Ambassador."

I put the phone down and looked at the Captain. "He wants to talk to the Ambassador at once."

The Captain gulped, but he left the room at a fast walk. I picked up the phone and listened until I heard a sleepy voice saying hello. Then I put it down.

I had to give General Roberts credit for one thing. When he moved, things started happening. Almost immediately we were escorted to the dining room and served some breakfast. By the time we had finished that, we were handed temporary papers allowing us to leave Finland. Then we were bustled into an official car and taken to an airport, where the big bomber was waiting. We were quickly passed by the officials and then boarded the plane. It took off at once.

We were up in the air only a few minutes when the pilot, a colonel, came back.

"Major March," he said, "General Roberts suggested that if we wanted to keep you happy we give you this." He handed me a bottle of brandy and went back up front.

Between the bottle of brandy and a few naps, we were in Washington almost before we had realized any amount of time had passed. We were met by a car and whisked away again. I could barely assure Irina I would see her soon when she vanished somewhere and I was left with the General.

I gave him my report. Then he told me that there probably wouldn't be any repercussions. James Hartwell would be brought to trial and negotiations were already under way to trade a Soviet prisoner for him. The Soviet government had announced that an American agent named Peter Miloff had been killed while trying to escape. By this time the old man in the Kremlin undoubtedly knew who Peter Miloff was, but they wouldn't change the story. The Brotherhood Coin Vending Company had been informed that their employee had been killed in Russia. That was lucky, because Zoubov's little heroin ring was too good a thing for the Syndicate and Georgi. He'd get word to them somehow, only we'd be ahead of him every step of the way.

General Roberts was so pleased he even gave me a pat on the back as he ushered me out and on my way to New York by another Air Force plane.

I finally ended up back in my own apartment on Perry Street. I showered, shaved, and changed clothes. I was tired, but I didn't feel like going to sleep, so I went out to the Blue

Mill and had a dry martini and talked to Alcino. Everything began to catch up with me after my second martini. I passed up dinner and went back to my apartment. The phone was ringing as I entered. I picked it up.

"Milo," she said. It was Irina. "They told me I could make one call to you. Thank you, Milo—and good night."

She hung up and I went to sleep.

AFTERWORD

The White-Haired Villain

The man who sat there and pulled his thousands of strings, stretching all over the world, had once been famous, but it was believed that he had died more than twenty years earlier in a Japanese prison. He was now in his seventies; his hair white and his face lined with the passions and cruelties that had filled his life.

There is something sinister about white-haired villains. In addition to Richard Sorge, the Milo March series boasts two others, both gangsters, in *Jade for a Lady* and *Green Grow the Graves.* They make me think of the notorious crime boss Whitey Bulger, who was captured in 2011 after sixteen years on the lam.

I had never heard of Richard Sorge and discovered quite by accident that he was a real person, and one of the most brilliant spies of the twentieth century. A Soviet agent during World War II, he was head of the Fourth Bureau, the forerunner of Russia's intelligence service, known as the GRU (which incidentally was linked to the hacking of the Democratic National Congress computer systems in 2016).

Sorge was sent to Japan in 1933 to establish a spy ring there. Following confessions by members of his ring (not because of betrayal by a particular girl, as stated in this novel), he was arrested in Tokyo in October 1941 (at age forty-nine—probably without white hair), and he was executed by hanging in November 1944. But it was not until 1964—four years before the publication of *Wild Midnight Falls*—that the Soviet Union acknowledged him, as recounted in the *New York Times:*

Under the heading "Tovarisch [Comrade] Richard Sorge," the Communist party newspaper, *Pravda,* eulogized the spy, now dead for 20 years. ... Viktor Maevskii, who wrote the article in *Pravda* acknowledging Sorge's existence and saluting him as one of Russia's most successful spies, also interviewed Sorge's mistress, Ishii Hanako, in Tokyo earlier this year. She took him to visit Sorge's grave in Tama cemetery, and provided him with a picture of the famous spy. Ishii Hanako is responsible for moving Sorge's body from the Sugamo prison cemetery to its present resting place, and for erecting an epitaph which reads, in Japanese: "Here lies a hero who sacrificed his life fighting against war and for world peace." [Chalmers Johnson, "Again the Sorge Case," *New York Times,* October 11, 1964]

Was there ever any mystery about whether Sorge had survived? It doesn't seem so. His lover Hanako identified his remains based on a leg injury and distinctive dental work. Considering the thoroughness with which Ken Crossen researched his novels, it's hard to believe he wouldn't have known that Sorge's death was a done deal. But if he did know, I wonder why he didn't give the character a fictional name.

Richard Sorge

I haven't seen any reviews of *Wild Midnight Falls* that were in on the secret of the great spy's true fate. Can it be that no one noticed this discrepancy?

In lightly editing this book for reissue, I considered changing "Richard Sorge" to a fictional name, but I thought I heard the faint rustling sound of Ken Crossen turning in his grave.

Let's just leave it that the reports of Richard Sorge's survival were greatly exaggerated.

Kendra Crossen Burroughs

ABOUT THE AUTHOR

Kendell Foster Crossen (1910–1981), the only child of Samuel Richard Crossen and Clo Foster Crossen, was born on a farm outside Albany in Athens County, Ohio—a village of some 550 souls in the year of this birth. His ancestors on his mother's side include the 19th-century songwriter Stephen Collins Foster ("Oh! Susanna"); William  Allen, founder of Allentown, Pennsylvania; and Ebenezer Foster, one of the Minute Men who sprang to arms at the Lexington alarm in April 1775.

Ken went to Rio Grande College on a football scholarship but stayed only one year. "When I was fairly young, I developed the disgusting habit of reading," says Milo March, and it seems Ken Crossen, too, preferred self-education. He loved literature and poetry; favorite authors included Christopher Marlowe and Robert Service. He also enjoyed participant sports and was a semi-pro fighter in the heavyweight class. He became a practicing magician and had a passion for chess.

After college Ken wrote several one-act plays that were produced in a small Cleveland theater. He worked in steel mills and Fisher Body plants. Then he was employed as an insurance investigator, or "claims adjuster," in Cleveland. But he left the job and returned to the theater, now as a performer: a tumbling clown in the Tom Mix Circus; a comic and carnival barker for a tent show, and an actor in a medicine show.

In 1935, Ken hitchhiked to New York City with a typewriter under his arm, and found work with the WPA Writers' Project, covering cricket for the *New York City Guidebook*. In 1936, he was hired by the Munsey Publishing Company as associate editor of the popular *Detective Fiction Weekly*. The company asked him to come up with a character to compete with The Shadow, and thus was born a unique superhero of pulps, comic books, and radio—The Green Lama, an American mystic trained in Tibetan Buddhism.

Crossen sold his first story, "The Aaron Burr Murder Case," to *Detective Fiction Weekly* in September 1939, but says he didn't begin to make a living from writing till 1941. He tried his hand at publishing true crime magazines, comics, and a picture magazine, without great success, so he set out for Hollywood. From his typewriter flowed hundreds of stories, short novels for magazines, scripts radio, television, and film, nonfiction articles. He delved into science fiction in the 1950s, starting with "Restricted Clientele" (February 1951). His dystopian novels *Year of Consent* and *The Rest Must Die* also appeared in this decade.

In the course of his career Ken Crossen acquired six pseud-onyms: Richard Foster, Bennett Barlay, Kent Richards, Clay Richards, Christopher Monig, and M.E. Chaber. The variety was necessary because different publishers wanted to reserve specific bylines for their own publications. Ken based "M.E. Chaber" on the Hebrew word for "author," *mechaber.*

In the early '50s, as M.E. Chaber, Crossen began to write a series of full-length mystery/espionage novels featuring Milo March, an insurance investigator. The first, *Hangman's Harvest,* was published in 1952. In all, there are twenty-two Milo March novels. One, *The Man Inside,* was made into a British film starring Jack Palance.

Most of Ken's characters were private detectives, and Milo was the most popular. Paperback Library reissued twenty-five Crossen titles in 1970–1971, with covers by Robert McGin-nis. Twenty were Milo March novels, four featured an insur-ance investigator named Brian Brett, and one was about CIA agent Kim Locke.

Crossen excelled at producing well-plotted entertainment with fast-moving action. His research skills were a strong asset, back when research meant long hours searching library microfilms and poring over street maps and hotel floorplans. His imagination took him to many international hot spots, although he himself never traveled abroad. Like Milo March, he hated flying ("When you've seen one cloud, you've seen them all").

Ken Crossen was married four times. With his first wife he had three children (Stephen, Karen, Kendra) and with his second a son (David). He lived in New York, Florida, Southern California, Nevada, and other parts of the country. Milo March moves from Denver to New York City after five books of the series, with an apartment on Perry Street in Greenwich Village; that's where Ken lived, too. His and Milo's favorite watering hole was the Blue Mill Tavern, a short walk from the apartment.

Ken Crossen was a combination of many of the traits of his different male characters: tough, adventuresome, with a taste for gin and shapely women. But perhaps the best observation was made in an obituary written by sci-fi writer Avram Davidson, who described Ken as a fundamentally gentle person who had been buffeted by many winds.